The Best Laid Plans

The
BEST
LAID
PLANS

M.E. ROSS

SECOND STORY Press

Canadian Cataloguing in Publication Data

Ross, M. E.
The best laid plans

ISBN 0-929005-73-2

I. Title.

PS8585.O77B4 1995   C813'.54   C95-931649-3
PR9199.3.R67B4 1995

Edited by Margaret E. Taylor

Second Story Press gratefully acknowledges the assistance of
The Canada Council and the Ontario Arts Council

Printed and bound in Canada

Published by
Second Story Press
720 Bathurst Street Suite 301
Toronto, Canada
M5S 2R4

For Erin

If wishes were horses

The Beginning

June 1987

IN THE BEGINNING there was Keely. And then there was Keely and Darla. And then there was Keely and Carolyn. And now there was just Keely again. Alone and back at the same old bar. She sighed and took a long pull off her beer bottle. The more things changed, the more they remained the same. She'd come full circle and ended up right back where she started from. She should have seen the handwriting on the wall. She'd only gotten what she deserved.

Keely glanced in the direction of the bar and the lone woman standing there smiled at her. She immediately returned her gaze to the beer bottle in front of her. The last thing she needed right now was for some twenty-year-old pup to think she was even remotely interested. That would be jumping from the frying pan into the fire, just like it would be to call Beth. Experience dictated that she leave that stone unturned. She'd made that mistake once before and look where that had gotten her; sitting in the same old tired bar, reciting all the worn-out clichés, asking the identical lame questions she'd asked herself a thousand times before.

She took a slug of her beer. The baby dyke at the bar smiled at her again and slid off her stool. Some serious evasive action was in order if she was going to escape the inevitable encounter. She picked up her beer and headed towards the phone as an avoidance manoeuvre, but when she got there she froze. She didn't know who to call. Carolyn was absolutely out of the question. She hadn't spoken to her in the month since she'd moved out and she wasn't about to now. And she didn't really have any friends. She'd always found being alone much more comfortable than the company of others. Beth popped into her mind again. She immediately dismissed even the possibility. Her admirer was now giving her the full stare. She picked up the receiver and dialled the only phone number she knew from memory.

"You have reached 555-1234," the disembodied voice of the answering machine greeted her. "I'm sorry to have missed your call. If you leave your name, number and date and time you called, I'll get back to you. Thanks for calling."

"Hi, Dar," Keely began hesitantly. "It's eight o'clock on Saturday and I was just calling to see if you wanted to meet me at the bar for a drink, but I guess I missed you. If you feel like it, why don't you give me a call sometime?" She faltered. She couldn't remember her new phone number. "I've moved onto Wolfe Street," she hurried before the machine cut her off. "It's Keely," she added for good measure. "Just in case you can't remember."

By the time she hung up the phone the sweet young thing was gone. Keely heaved a sigh of relief and ordered another beer. Thirty seconds later she realized her error when the woman stepped out of the washroom.

"You must be new in town!" she gushed enthusiastically.

Keely cringed. Life really was just one big cliché.

"Beth's here," Louise announced.

Jane turned from the bar and scanned the crowded room. Finally she located Louise's ex-lover sitting at a corner table, deeply engrossed in conversation with someone she'd never seen before.

"And look who she's with," she noted.

Jane shrugged. "I don't know her at all."

"Her name is Keely Logan," she relayed in disgust.

Louise's tone set Jane's radar off. She watched Louise coolly observing the pair, preparing herself for the latest rendition of Beth's hopeless attraction to losers. Keely didn't look like a loser to Jane, but then most of the others didn't seem to be either.

"I guess Carolyn must have finally come to her senses and dumped her," Louise happily concluded.

"Carolyn?" Jane questioned.

"Carolyn Sinclair," she provided. "The psych prof."

"So you know her from the university then," Jane surmised.

"Hardly," she chortled. "She runs a two-bit construction company with her brother."

Jane waited for more information but none came. Gossiping was usually one of Louise's favourite pastimes. Her silence on the topic was more than strange. Jane decided her radar was right. The peace that had recently broken out between Louise and Beth was once again shaky.

"Let's get out of here," Louise growled. "All of a sudden it feels very crowded."

"Would you like to come up and see my etchings?"

Beth smiled. Now her quarry was even more irresistible. Butch exterior, marshmallow interior and a sense of humour too. It was almost too good to be true.

"No, eh?" Keely smirked. "How about a round of chesterfield rugby then?"

Beth laughed. She still couldn't tell if she was kidding or not, and Keely's slight smile and twinkling eyes weren't giving a thing away. There was only one way to find out what was really behind the offer. She shut off the car.

Keely stumbled halfway up the back stairs and fumbled

getting her key in the lock. She was obviously more loaded than Beth had originally thought.

"Make yourself at home," Keely invited and promptly disappeared into the bathroom.

Beth took off her jacket and surveyed the small attic apartment. The lone piece of furniture in the living-room area was a futon which no doubt doubled as a bed. She opted to remain standing in the kitchen.

Keely emerged from the bathroom and zigzagged her way to the sofa, tripping over the leg of the coffee table before literally falling onto her destination. She managed to right herself into a sitting position and grinned at Beth again.

"Aren't you going to join me on the playing field?" she tossed out.

Beth hesitated. As much as she wanted to take Keely up on her offer, her less-than-sober state made the prospect of the game progressing very far less than likely.

"Well?" Keely asked again.

Beth picked up her jacket. "Maybe another time?" she opted.

"Hey! Not fair!" Keely protested. "You can't go yet. You haven't given me a chance to turn on the wit and charm."

Beth smiled and put her jacket over the kitchen chair again. She wasn't about to object a second time. She crossed the room to sit down beside her. Keely dropped her arm from the back of the sofa to Beth's shoulders in an attempt to get the game under way. Beth turned to smile at her and Keely landed the kiss on cue. It began almost innocently and then seemingly out of nowhere turned into a passionate exchange of oral calisthenics ending with Keely sprawled half on top of Beth. And then she just lay there with her face buried in Beth's neck.

"Keely?" Beth checked.

"Uh-huh."

"Are you okay?"

"Fucked if I know," she sighed.

Beth rubbed the back of her neck. "Do you want me to go?"

Keely struggled and finally sat up, putting her head in her hands. "I'm sorry," she apologized. "I'm really drunk and fucked up right now."

Beth sat up too. "Do you want me to go?" she repeated.

All was silent on the Keely front.

"Come on then," Beth urged her. "Why don't we pull out the bed?"

"Beth ... I don't think I can ...."

"I know," she chuckled. She was never operating under the delusion that Keely could. "I thought maybe you'd like to get some sleep?"

Keely nodded and stood while Beth unfolded the futon. She collapsed back on it and was instantly asleep. Beth covered her with a blanket and let herself out, locking the door behind her, smiling all the while. She'd let Keely get away this time, but next time her quarry wouldn't be so lucky.

"The two of you certainly looked cosy last night."

Beth rolled her eyes. She wished she hadn't bothered to answer the phone. The tone was unmistakable. Louise did not approve.

"So where do you know Keely from?"

"She's my new upstairs neighbour."

"She's the one you've been going on and on about for the last two weeks?"

"Uh-huh," Beth confirmed warily. "Where do you know her from and why didn't you come over and say hi?"

"I didn't want to interrupt."

Louise was selling but Beth wasn't buying.

"So?"

"So what?" Beth goaded her.

"Last night? What happened?"

"Nothing much," she tormented her.

"Come on, Beth!"

"I told you. Nothing happened. We had a couple of drinks together and she was really drunk and I drove her home. That's it."

"Oh ... you're not interested in her, are you?"

"She's an interesting person," she deftly sidestepped.

"Sexually, I mean."

"I'm not sure," she dodged evasively.

"Oh ... are you going to see her again?"

"I expect so," Beth laughed. "We're neighbours, for heaven's sake."

"Oh ... you're still coming to Jane's for dinner and movies tonight, aren't you?"

Beth sighed. "Sure. I guess."

"Okay then. See you around six."

Louise hung up the phone in a full-blown snit. Beth was really interested in Keely and just wasn't admitting it.

"So what's up?" Jane asked the almost unnecessary question.

"Beth's interested in Keely."

Jane nodded. She'd figured as much.

Louise continued on with her scowl and then brightened into a smile. "We should invite that woman you went to law school with over tonight," she decided.

"Rebecca? Why? I thought we were only having a little get-together."

"We are," Louise confirmed. "Didn't you say Rebecca split up with her lover a few months back?"

Jane nodded.

"It's perfect. Meg and Sophie and Beth and Rebecca."

"It sounds like you're matchmaking," Jane realized.

"I am. I'm sure Beth and Rebecca will hit it off. I don't know why I didn't think of this sooner."

Jane did. It was because Keely wasn't in the picture. "I don't know," she attempted to discourage the whole thing. "Rebecca doesn't really seem like Beth's type."

"Exactly!" Louise concurred. "At least, not the type she's usually into. She's bright and well-educated and a professional. Maybe if Beth met somebody a little more appropriate for her, she'd forget all about Keely Logan."

Jane tried to imagine what Rebecca and Beth would think of one another. Rebecca would probably be interested in Beth, but she doubted very much it would be mutual. Rebecca was just too stuffy.

"Call her," Louise directed, her mind made up.

Jane sighed in defeat. Her only hope now was that Rebecca was busy.

Keely woke up in a fog, unsure of her surroundings. And then it all came flooding back to her, or at least what she could remember of it. She stumbled out of bed and into the kitchen to make a pot of coffee, trying to reconstruct the night before. She remembered calling Beth and that Beth had driven her home, but the only other event she could honestly recollect was necking on the sofa. They didn't sleep together, she was sure of that, but she had absolutely no idea how they'd even wound up in her apartment or how she'd ended up alone. She shook her head at the entire situation. She hated getting stupid drunk! She only ended up doing really stupid things that she always regretted the next day, and last night was no exception. When she was sober she knew well enough to leave any involvement with Beth alone, but after a dozen or so beers she'd lost sight of how much Beth resembled Carolyn. Beth was a professor too. English instead of psychology, admittedly, but nonetheless an academic and, unless Keely missed her bet, she was also the marrying kind. She radiated it. Keely shuddered at the thought. The last thing she needed in her life was a Carolyn-clone, and yet last night she'd almost done it to herself again.

The phone rang, interrupting her latest round of Keely-bashing. She hesitated to answer it, afraid it might be Beth, but in the end she picked it up anyway.

"Hi there, stranger," the familiar, sultry voice cooed to her.

Keely winced, instantly reminded of yet another bone-headed thing she'd done the night before.

"I'm sorry I was out when you called. I would have liked to have met you for that drink. But it sure was nice to come home and find your voice waiting for me."

An entire flock of butterflies fluttered into Keely's stomach at Dar's intonation. "I was sorry I missed you too," she replied, switching hands on the phone to wipe her sweaty palm. "Maybe we can do it another time?"

"I'd like that," Dar's voice purred to her. "How's this afternoon for you?"

Keely's heart rate escalated. As far as she was concerned next year would be too soon.

"Say in about an hour?"

Keely swallowed. "Sure," she replied, full of false brava-do. "The house number is 530. Top floor, around back."

"See you then."

Keely stood holding the receiver with her second, now equally sweaty hand, listening to the dial tone. Dar's tone left little to the imagination. Her call last night had defi-nitely set the wheels in motion and, ready or not, she was about to step back on the roller coaster again.

Beth took the back stairs two at time. She hadn't laid eyes on Keely all day, and borrowing a couple of beers on a hot Sunday afternoon was as good an excuse as any. Beth knocked gently on the screen door in case she was still asleep.

"Just a second," Keely's voice replied.

The inside door was slightly ajar and there was soft music playing. Beth's wait turned into a minute and moved on into the two or three zone before a very dishevelled Keely popped her head between the doors.

"Hi," she smiled nervously. "What's up?"

"I was wondering if you had a couple of beers I could borrow? I'm all out and I'd kill for one right now."

"Sure," Keely nodded. "Just a sec."

She disappeared inside, leaving a disappointed Beth standing on the landing. She was hoping for an invitation in, but from her vantage point she could see that the bed was pulled down. Keely had been sleeping after all. She looked a little more closely and cringed. If it was sleeping Keely was doing, she wasn't doing it alone.

Keely filled the doorway again to hand her the now urgently needed brews. Beth felt herself blush beet red, which of course only caused Keely to do the same. Describing the moment as awkward would be an understatement.

"Thanks," Beth whimpered feebly and slithered down the stairs. She knew there had to be a good rock to hide under somewhere.

"Was it as good as it used to be?" Darla teased.

"Better," she sighed.

Darla slid her hand slowly up the inside of Keely's thigh. "Didn't I tell you Carolyn wouldn't hold a candle to me?"

"You did," Keely agreed.

Darla's finger dipped into the waiting wetness. Keely closed her eyes.

"Did you miss me?"

Keely's kiss resoundingly confirmed that she had, and in a major big way. Darla smiled. She'd missed her Keely too.

Beth escaped from Jane's at eleven-thirty. She was furious! The moment she'd arrived, she'd smelled the set-up. Louise had it planned perfectly. A quaint little evening for six: Louise and Jane, Meg and Sophie, and Beth and Rebecca!

Rebecca! Beth shook her head. The woman hung on her every word all night long, clearly enthralled with her. She could hardly even go to the bathroom alone! And she was so stuffy and downright boring. All Rebecca wanted to talk about was law school and her new BMW. And the scariest part was that she'd asked for her phone number when she'd left! The woman couldn't seem to take a hint. She certainly had tried hard enough, Beth had to give her that, but she had two strikes against her from the start: being both a friend of Jane's and somebody Louise deemed appropriate. The bottom line was it would have taken a miracle for Beth to have been interested in her.

Beth's humour plummeted even further when she pulled into the driveway to find a black jeep parked behind Keely's truck, the same black jeep she'd seen earlier parked on the street. Its licence plate made it unmistakable. It read BIG TOY. Beth shook her head. Obviously it belonged to the dark-haired woman who was probably still in Keely's bed. From the length of her stay, Beth speculated there was a pretty good chance the label referred not only to the vehicle but to its owner too.

Brock was shocked to walk into the job shack and find his twin sister already there, not that she was usually late, but she was certainly never early. At least not this early.

"So what's up with you?"

"I need to talk to you."

He smiled and waited for her to tell him something he didn't already know.

"I think I might have done something really stupid on the weekend," Keely confessed.

"You slept with the neighbour," he surmised from last week's major topic of conversation.

"Not that stupid," Keely disputed. "Or at least I don't think so," she reconsidered. "I saw Dar yesterday."

Stupidity was in the eye of the beholder as far as Brock was concerned. Doing the neighbour was far less complicated for his sister than getting re-involved with Darla could ever be!

"We ended up sleeping together," she further illuminated.

"You what?" he sputtered. "What did you do that for?"

"Because I was lonely and I was horny and because she's good in bed!" she reacted defensively. "Okay?"

Brock sighed. Keely exasperated him. She never seemed to learn, even the hard way. "Are you going to see her again?"

"I don't see any reason not to," she shrugged.

"I thought you didn't need complicated right now?" he reminded her.

"This doesn't have to be complicated."

"Come on, Keely. You know you don't believe that.

When it comes to you and Darla, nothing's simple."

"It's going to be different this time," she decided.

"Oh. I see. She's ready to settle down and play house, now is she?"

"No!" Keely replied defiantly. "This time I don't want to play house either."

"Yet," he added drily. "History has a way of repeating itself."

"I sure hope so," Keely grinned. "Dar and I had some pretty good times together."

"And some pretty lousy ones too."

"I'm not going to make the same mistakes twice," she reassured him. "I know what I'm doing."

Brock shook his head at his sister. If she wanted to hit her head against the same wall again, there was nothing he or anyone else could do about it. Keely was as stubborn as a mule and sometimes just about as stupid too.

Beth wrote her Monday off as one of the worst in history. Her morning had started out on the low note of the annual departmental curriculum meeting, which had dragged on and on as only academic meetings can, making her late for her luncheon date with Louise, and from that point forward her day had only gone downhill. Beth had made the mistake of bringing up the topic of Rebecca in an effort to explain why she was so upset about being set up, but Louise had immediately seized the opportunity to extol the woman's many virtues instead. And then, as if things weren't bad enough already, Louise had ended their get-together with the less-than-thrilling announcement that she and her dearly beloved Janey were moving in together. Beth sighed and shook her head. Whatever it was that her usually overly critical ex-lover saw in the woman totally defied explanation. In Beth's eyes, Jane the Pain qualified as nothing short of the most boring woman on earth. But she hadn't bothered to say anything. It would have been a waste of breath anyway.

"Hi, sweetie!" Wally cheerily called to her as she sorted through her mail. "Isn't it simply a marvellous day?"

Beth smiled despite her filthy mood.

"Come and see," he invited her, getting up from his knees. "I thought I'd put pansies in again this year," he went on merrily. "They always seem so appropriate, don't you think?"

Beth laughed. "Totally," she agreed.

He slipped his arm through hers and took her on a tour of his freshly planted garden. "So what do you think?" he enthused.

"I think they're even more divine than last year," she approved completely. "The best ever."

"Do you think so?" he beamed. "I wasn't going to do it and then I thought, No! You get out there and plant those pansies, just like you always have. Nicky would have wanted it that way. Don't you think?"

Beth nodded and got back to being depressed again, this time for Wally. His lover of almost ten years had died of AIDS last summer, and even though he'd never said anything, Beth knew damned well her landlord and best friend was just waiting for the day when he'd get sick too.

"So, have you met our new housemate?" he brightly inquired.

Beth nodded and sighed.

"And?"

"And you didn't tell me she was a dyke."

"Oh, didn't I?" he feigned innocence. "It must have slipped my mind."

Beth smiled. "I'll bet."

"Pretty cute, eh?" he nudged her.

Beth just shrugged. What difference did it make what she thought anyway? After her inadvertent discovery that Keely was involved with someone else, the whole thing was irrelevant. Under normal circumstances she would have discussed her woes with Louise, but she had remained silent out of self-preservation. Another lecture on the appropriateness thing was something she could do without. What she really needed was an unbiased opinion, something a little hard to find in such a small community. Conservative old London, Ontario, was far better known for its picturesque tree-lined streets than for its out lesbian population and sometimes it felt just a little too much like a fish bowl. Beth once again caught herself longing for the anonymity offered just two hours east in Toronto.

"Is something wrong, sweetie?"

Unless, of course, that unbiased opinion was six feet tall, all dressed in lavender and standing right in front of her.

"You just sit down and tell old Wally all about it," he urged her, sitting on the steps and patting her spot next to him. "Now what's wrong?"

"It's about our new housemate," she began, and then proceeded to launch into what she intended to be the *Reader's Digest* condensed version. "So should I leave well enough alone?" she finally ended her longer-than-intended rendition.

Wally pursed his lips in silent contemplation. He didn't like giving advice on matters of the heart too hastily. "I think not," he decided.

"But what about this other woman?" she protested.

"For all you know, she's just a one-date wonder," he pointed out.

Beth scowled. One-date wonders didn't usually last all afternoon and all night too. "So what should I do, Wally?" she whined.

"Well, it seems to me the answer is patently obvious," he grinned. "If the mountain won't come to Muhammad, Muhammad should go to the mountain."

"Huh?"

"Ask her out," he giggled.

"Do you think so?"

He nodded. "I wouldn't say no to you," he stated with certainty.

Beth smiled appreciatively. She didn't know what she'd do without her Wally.

Dar's urgent phone call came right around quitting time. She made Keely promise to come over as soon as she could. Permission was denied for her to go home first to shower and change on the grounds that it was an emergency. Keely pulled into her driveway not ten minutes later, dog-tired and sweaty and worried. Darla dashed out of the side door of her office to join her.

"So what couldn't wait?"

"Come and see," Darla urged her.

Keely followed her into the garage apprehensively.

"This!" she beamed.

"It's a motorcycle," Keely stated.

"It's not just a motorcycle," Darla corrected her. "It's a Harley."

"I can see that."

"Isn't it great?" she enthused.

Keely shrugged. This was the emergency?

"I bought it this afternoon."

"Why?"

"Because it's fun," Darla laughed.

"But you don't even know how to drive it," Keely argued.

"Sure I do. I used to have one when I was in school. I

rode it all the time. Even in the winter sometimes."

Keely shook her head at herself. Nothing about Dar should still surprise her.

"Let's go for a spin," she suggested eagerly.

"No way," Keely flatly refused. Dar's car driving was scary enough. The thought of getting on a motorcycle behind her was positively terrorizing.

"Okay," she gave in. "We'll go after dinner then."

Keely smiled. Obviously her staying for dinner was a foregone conclusion, and now that she was here she wasn't about to argue. She followed Darla up the flight of steps to the back deck, where the champagne for the toast to the new motorcycle just happened to be chilled and waiting. Keely indulged in a couple of glasses before being sent off to shower and change into the clean clothes in her size that had somehow just magically appeared on the bed. Keely's smile grew when she rejoined Darla on the deck. The intimate table for two was already set.

Dinner was everything Keely knew it would be and was followed by the predictable after-dinner brandy. Dar hadn't missed a thing. She was definitely up to her old tricks again, and Keely relaxed into the familiarity, happy to take a leisurely stroll down memory lane. She remembered building the very deck they were sitting on as if it was yesterday. The day they'd finished, they'd had a late-night barbeque and then dragged out a sleeping bag and made love under the stars.

"What are you so busy thinking about?" Darla inquired.

Keely smiled. "I was remembering when we built this deck."

"It was just about the same time of year," Darla joined her in the memory.

"Nine years ago this week," Keely answered with certainty. "Just before my twenty-sixth birthday."

"That's right," Darla recalled. "I gave you a watch."

Keely extended her wrist. Darla took her hand to examine the timepiece. She was surprised that Keely still wore it. The crystal was all scratched and the casing was spattered with paint.

"Do you remember the inscription on the back?" Keely wondered.

"Of course I do," she assured her. "It says, 'Love always, Dar,' and I still feel that way."

Keely held her gaze evenly. Darla smiled and got to her feet. Keely's eyes followed her towards the patio door longingly.

"Where are you going?" she called after her.

"To find that old sleeping bag," she replied.

Keely laughed. Brock was right. Sometimes history did repeat itself.

Keely polished off the last of her French fries and looked up to find Beth smiling at her yet again. She was beginning to get the distinct impression that tonight's impromptu invitation to go out for a burger and a beer wasn't any more spur of the moment than Dar's summons yesterday. In fact, unless Keely missed her guess, she was on a date. She pushed her plate aside in favour of her beer, silently cursing her own stupidity. After all, what was the woman supposed to think? She had kissed her, if not more, less than seventy-two hours before. Keely promptly signalled the waitress for another drink.

Beth gave up while she was behind and let Keely enjoy her fourth beer in silence. Things were not going well. Keely had barely said more than a dozen words the entire meal and her major focus seemed to be her own split and blackened right thumbnail. It seemed futile to further torture her.

Keely viewed it as a merciful thing when the bill finally arrived. Beth, on the other hand, started to panic. By the time she pulled into the driveway it was abundantly clear to her that unless she did something, and probably something drastic, their evening together was about to end just as it had begun, with the two of them nothing more than awkward acquaintances. But as to what that something might be, Beth had absolutely no idea.

"Thanks for suggesting dinner," Keely filled the torturous silence. "I had a good time."

Beth smiled at her blatant lie.

"Well ... good night," she offered awkwardly.

"Aren't you going to invite me up for a round of chesterfield rugby again?" she seized the opening.

Keely winced. "I didn't really say that, did I?"

"You also asked me if I'd like to see your etchings."

"I didn't," Keely cringed. "I can be such an asshole when I'm drunk."

"Oh, I don't know," she countered. "I thought you were kind of cute."

Keely grinned sheepishly. Now she was really nervous.

Beth knew what she had to do. It was without doubt time for Muhammad to go to the mountain again. She leaned over and kissed her, and although Keely kissed her back, she didn't do so very convincingly. As far as Beth was concerned, that confirmed it.

"You're involved with someone else," she prompted.

"Sort of," Keely waffled.

"So something between us would be out of the question because of that?"

"No, not because of that," Keely replied with a sigh. Dar probably couldn't care less if she slept with Beth or anyone else for that matter. She never had.

"You don't find me attractive," Beth decided.

"No. I do. Really," she hurriedly assured her. "I find you extremely attractive."

"So what is it then?"

Keely turned and looked out the passenger window, trying to find the right words. "I'm just not up for anything complicated right now," she finally managed.

"This doesn't have to be complicated."

"Oh yes it does."

"Why?"

"Because we live right on top of each other."

"So what?"

Keely took a deep breath. She wasn't making this easy.

"Keely?"

"I'm not looking to get married," she came out with it.

"Neither am I," Beth answered with certainty. "I just thought maybe we could have something nice."

Keely turned to look at Beth and Muhammad promptly kissed the mountain again. Keely gave up and gave in, kissing her Carolyn-clone paranoia good-bye.

Darla arrived in the nick of time. Keely heard her roar up from behind just as she was locking up the job shack for the night.

"Want a ride on my motorcycle, little girl?"

Keely laughed. "What's that? Your new line for the summer?"

"Sure. What do you think?"

"Not bad," Keely conceded.

Darla held out the helmet and leather jacket she'd brought her. "Get ready," she instructed. "Hop on."

"I can't Dar. I'm supposed to meet Brock to play squash."

"That sounds pretty boring compared to what I had planned for us."

"And what's that?"

"A bike ride to the lake and a moonlight boat cruise with some friends in Grand Bend."

Dar was right. Squash with Brock did sound dull by comparison.

"Tell him you got a better offer. I'll make it worth your while," she promised seductively.

"I'm filthy dirty. I need to shower and change."

"Not to worry. I've got everything you need right here," Darla patted the saddlebags. "You can shower at my friends' place."

"I really shouldn't," Keely wavered.

"That will make it all the more fun then, won't it?" she countered. "Hurry up now. Call him and tell him you're not coming."

Keely turned around and went back inside the job shack. She begged off due to exhaustion. It wasn't totally a lie after being up half the night with Beth, but she still felt guilty. She shook her head at herself. She wasn't sure who to be more annoyed with, herself for giving in so easily or Dar for knowing how to get to her so very well.

"So how did it go?" he wanted to know.

"The date?"

Wally nodded.

"Not so great," Beth tortured him.

"I'm sorry, sweetie," he tried to console her.

"But after we got home, now that was a different story," she beamed.

"Why you little sneak," he chided her. "Come on now. Give me details."

"Well, you know how the first time things are usually all clumsy and awkward and don't turn out so great?"

"Are they?" Wally teased. "It's been so long I can't remember."

Beth laughed. "For me they usually are."

"But?" he prompted her.

"But they weren't," she grinned from ear to ear. "We actually managed to even laugh about the whole thing."

"That bad, eh?" he chuckled.

"It was terrible," she giggled. "So terrible we're going to do it again tomorrow night."

Brock finally cornered his sister at lunch. They hadn't spoken all morning and he was beginning to get the feeling that she'd been avoiding him. And she looked like a bag of shit, all tired and hobbling around like an old woman.

"You've looked better," he remarked. "Are you feeling okay?"

"I'm all right. Just tired."

"I thought you were going to get some sleep last night."

Keely realized that Brock was onto her. It was time to fess up. "I ended up going to the beach with Dar," she admitted.

"What a surprise," he replied caustically.

"She got a new motorcycle and really wanted me to come along on her first run."

"She's got a motorcycle?"

"Uh-huh. She just bought it."

He shook his head. Darla's overgrown adolescent behaviour hadn't changed a bit.

"And then we ended up coming back in the pouring rain."

"So that explains the hobbling around," he logically concluded.

"Partly," she smirked. "That and making out on a damned deck chair."

Brock shook his head again. "I thought she might have grown out of that phase."

"Not Dar. She'll never grow up."

"She's got to be even more crippled than you are. She's getting up there," he remembered.

"Forty-seven," Keely provided. "But she's just fine. Fresh as a daisy."

"So she stayed overnight again?"

Keely nodded.

"Sounds like she's around a lot these days," he disapproved entirely.

Keely shrugged. "You know Dar. She'll be around every day for a week and then disappear for a while."

Brock knew better than to believe that of this week anyway. There was no way Darla would miss an opportunity for celebration like Keely's birthday.

"The two of you have plans for *our* birthday, no doubt," he presumed. "Are we still on for dinner tomorrow or are you going to stand me up for that one too?"

"No. I'm not going to stand you up," she promised. "Dar and I are going to get together later."

"Well, get some sleep," he advised. "Go home tonight and crash."

"I'd really love to," she fantasized. "But I can't."

"Dear Darla again?" he asked, incredulous at his sister's stamina for punishment.

"No," she casually replied. "Actually I've got a date with Beth."

"Beth? Who's Beth?"

"My downstairs neighbour."

"When did you find time in your busy schedule for the complicated thing?" she awed him completely.

"Earlier this week."

"And was it awful and complicated?"

"No," Keely reflected. "Actually it was really nice and quite simple."

"So are you going to continue seeing her?"

"I hope so," she grinned.

"What about Darla?"

Keely shrugged. "I'll see her too."

"Does she know about Darla?"

"Uh-huh."

"And does Darla know about her?"

"Yes."

"And it's okay with both of them?" he asked incredulously. "Darla's not jealous?"

"Doesn't seem to be," Keely answered. "In fact she wants to meet Beth or at least see her. She says she's curious to see what type of woman appeals to me now."

"You're kidding," he laughed nervously.

"No, I'm not," she assured him. "Can you believe that woman?"

Right at that moment Brock would have believed just about anything of either Darla or his sister.

Beth hung up the phone, disgusted with herself. Her mother had managed to do it to her yet again. She'd been reduced from a grown woman of thirty-seven to a guilty four-year-old in under thirty seconds. All she'd done was turn down her mother's rather insistent summons to come and visit for the weekend. After all, her mother had reminded her several times, it was Father's Day. The problem was it was also Keely's birthday tomorrow, and even though she was already busy they had made plans to celebrate on Saturday. Somehow between the two it was a non-decision.

Beth rolled over to face Keely again and was instantly

even further annoyed by her mother and her untimely interruption. Keely was sound asleep.

Keely eased into consciousness alone in bed. Their lovemaking had left her as it so often did, all soft and sleepy, and as usual, Dar had ended up too full of energy to stay in bed. She rolled onto her back and looked at her new watch again. It really was an incredibly thoughtful gift. Dar was getting sentimental in her old age. She'd even had it inscribed the same way.

Keely closed her eyes and drifted contentedly to the soft music in the background. Everything was so familiar: the room, the ever-present soft duvet and the scent of Dar and their lovemaking. It was as if she'd gone back seven or eight years in time. Back to when everything was so much easier and less complicated.

She reluctantly made herself get up and put on the robe laid out for her at the foot of the bed. She found Dar exactly where she knew she would, sitting in front of the fire sipping brandy.

"You're finally awake," she greeted her. "You slept a long time."

Keely yawned and sat on the floor beside her. "You wore me out."

"Poor baby," Darla teased. "Over the hill at thirty-five."

Keely smiled back at her. Dar's cheeks were still flushed from their shared passion. She'd never looked more beautiful.

"So have you gotten over being mad at me for kidnapping you?"

"I have, but I'm not sure Brock will."

Darla laughed. "It will give him all the more reason to hate me."

"He doesn't hate you, Dar."

Darla raised an eyebrow. She begged to differ, but there was no point in getting into it again.

"I love my new watch," Keely told her.

Darla smiled. "And I love you."

Keely lay back on the floor, once again lapsing into a time warp.

"What are you thinking about?"

"About being here with you tonight. It's just like old times."

"Yes, it is," Darla agreed.

"Sometimes I just wish ...." Keely's voice trailed off. It seemed pointless to finish her sentence. She already knew what Dar's reaction would be: if wishes were horses then beggars would ride.

"Keely, Keely, Keely," Darla scolded her affectionately. "I thought you'd given up that old fantasy. You said yourself from your experience with Carolyn that living with someone isn't everything it's cracked up to be."

"Never mind," Keely shook her head at the futility.

"We have so much," Darla tried again. "Why can't you just let things be and enjoy them while they're happening?"

It was a good question, and one Keely had asked herself ten thousand times before.

"Let's not do this tonight. Can't we forgo the annual birthday fight for one year?" Darla attempted a tease.

To Keely, their conversation felt like a script from the past. Once again they were waging the same old war about their living arrangements. Sure the words were different, but the outcome was an inevitability. Some things never changed.

August

BETH SAT ACROSS the table from Louise, suffering through their ritual weekly luncheon. Louise was blathering on about living with Jane and Janey's new car and Jane's this and Janey's that. She stifled another yawn. She'd hoped that once they'd moved in together the ever-boring topic of Jane would come up less frequently. So much for that theory.

"How come you're so tired?" Louise finally noticed.

"I was up late last night."

"Anybody I know?" she wanted the scoop.

"Yes, as a matter of fact," Beth approached the issue head on. "Keely."

Louise scowled. Beth hadn't mentioned her in weeks. She'd mistakenly assumed the fascination with Keely had passed. "Are you sleeping with her?" she came right out and asked.

"We have a few times," Beth grossly understated the situation.

"How involved are you?"

"I don't know," Beth hedged evasively. "I mean we're friends and the sex is nice, but it's nothing deep or anything."

Louise heaved an inward sigh of relief. By the sound of things, Beth's interlude with Keely wasn't going to amount to anything. There was no reason to believe that this little fling wouldn't follow the typical pattern of Beth's other involvements. They'd have some hot, sexy thing for a few weeks and then Beth would fall out of lust with her and

Keely Logan would take her rightful place in Beth's life. Just another in a long line of inappropriate, short-term lovers.

"You don't like Keely," Beth observed.

"No, it's not that really," she bobbed and weaved. "I just worry about you. Keely did just split up with Carolyn a couple of months ago," she pointed out.

"I am well aware of that, Louise."

"I know you are," she backed off sweetly. "I just wish you'd meet somebody more stable and settle down."

"And just where am I supposed to meet this someone? So far, sitting around singing, 'Someday my princess will come' hasn't worked."

"How about Rebecca?"

"Oh Jesus, Louise. Not her again!"

"Okay, okay," she relented. "So the two of you didn't hit it off right away."

"Read my lips! I don't find anything about the woman the least bit attractive."

"I think you might if you gave her a chance."

"No! And I mean it. No more set-ups with Rebecca or anyone else for that matter. Okay?"

"I just want you to be happy," she offered amiably.

More than anything, Beth wanted to believe her.

"You haven't forgotten about *our* party on Saturday, have you?" she swapped topics abruptly.

Beth shook her head. "I'll be there," she grudgingly conceded.

Louise smiled. She'd have to make sure Jane remembered to invite Rebecca. Surely Beth would recognize her perfect princess with just one more look.

"We are not taking the damned bike!" she restated adamantly. "It's going to rain."

"Oh, it is not!" she countered.

"Yes, it is."

"No, it's not!" Darla proclaimed.

But it did. The downpour started around midnight, right about the time Dar was finally ready to leave. It didn't last all that long, just long enough to soak them to the skin. By the time they arrived, Keely was chilled to the bone and furious, and Darla knew it too. She poured Keely a hot bath to defrost her, heated her thoroughly with a massage that was nothing short of steamy and then took her to her bed to finish wheedling her forgiveness completely.

Beth rounded the front corner of the house in search of a Wally diversion. She was sick and tired of feeling sorry for herself. He'd know what to do.

"Hi, Wally," she called. "How are you doing?"

"Oh," he heaved a huge and thunderous sigh. "Okay, I guess."

Beth leaned against the porch railing to take a closer look at him. He looked every day of his nearly fifty years and then some, and it just wasn't like him to be drinking all alone. Something was obviously very wrong.

"It's been exactly a year since Nicky's been gone. Sometimes it's hard to believe it's been that long."

"It sure is," Beth commiserated, feeling badly for not having put two and two together sooner.

"I was just thinking about something he said to me, a day or two before he died," he shared.

"What's that?"

"Crazy bastard," he smiled. "There he was, sick as a dog, literally on his death bed and he looked up at me and smiled and said, 'You live by the sword, you die by the sword.' Can you believe that? The man was dying and there he was trying to cheer me up with his crazy black humour."

Beth reached over and rested her hand on Wally's knee as he silently cried.

"I don't think I'll ever love anyone the way I loved that man," he sniffled.

Beth didn't know what to say.

"Look at me," Wally wiped his tears away. "A crazy old fag sitting here feeling sorry for myself. So how are you?" he redirected the conversation. "No hot date tonight?"

"It's BIG TOY night," she pissed and moaned. "For the second night in a row."

"What is the Other Woman's name anyway? You never did say."

"Beats me," she shrugged. "I told Keely right up front that I didn't want to know anything about her."

"Playing ostrich, are we?" he teased.

"Something like that," she agreed.

Wally fell silent again, lost in his thoughts.

"Wally?"

"Hmm?"

"Do you think it would be a mistake for me to tell Keely that I love her?" she sought his sage advice.

"Telling someone that you love them, when you really do of course, is never a mistake," he quietly replied. "Do you?"

"Yeah," she sighed. "I do."

Wally smiled at his confused dear friend. "Care to join me for a margarita?" he inquired.

Beth brightened immediately. She'd thought he'd never ask.

Brock watched the crew watch Darla drop Keely off. It was bad enough that she came in three-and-a-half hours late, but the little display in the jeep was more than he could take. He waited for Darla to pull away and strode purposefully towards her.

"Good morning," she chirped cheerily in hopes of disarming him.

"Good afternoon, don't you mean? I'm fed up with your being late," he fumed. "And no more of that crap, either!" he dictated. "There's no need for you and your girl-friend to entertain the crew!"

Her smile broadened into a full-fledged grin.

"And wipe that smile off your face," her indestructible good mood further irritated him. "We've got work to do."

Keely lay with her head on Beth's stomach and her legs over the side of the bed, catching maximum breeze from the fan. It was two-thirty in the morning and she had to get up for work in three-and-a-half hours. She hated working Saturdays nearly as much as she hated the heat and humidity.

"I think we've died and gone to hell," she suggested.

"Oh, I don't know," Beth begged to differ. "Not all that long ago it felt like heaven to me."

Keely laughed and unstuck her left shoulder from Beth's right thigh.

"What are you doing tomorrow night?" Beth broached.

"Nothing that I know of. Why?"

"Would you come to a party with me?"

Keely shrugged. "Sure. I guess."

"Good!" Beth celebrated. "I'm afraid if I show up without a date, Jane and Louise will sick Rebecca on me again."

"Who's Rebecca?"

"This very strange woman Louise keeps trying to set me up with."

Keely shook her head. She still couldn't get over the fact that Beth and the Wicked Bitch of the West were once lovers, even if it was a million years ago. And now Louise had actually found yet another poor sucker to move in with.

"What's Jane like?" she wondered aloud.

"She's a very boring, extremely serious thirty-year-old who has all the personality of a tropical plant."

Keely cracked up.

"A decorative palm," she further specified. "All light and fluffy, just hanging around taking up space."

Now Keely was howling so hard she was making waves in the waterbed.

"You'll get to meet her tomorrow," Beth warned.

"They'll be at the party?"

"It's at their place. It's to celebrate the joyous event of their co-habitation. We'll go late and leave early," Beth promised.

Keely sighed. Beth was right. They weren't in hell. Not yet, anyway. That pleasure was being delayed until tomorrow evening.

Afternoon sex always felt decadent to Keely. Actually sex with Dar anytime felt decadent, she reconsidered, as she lay in bed watching her dress.

"I hate to ravage and run," Darla grinned. "But I've got a client to see."

Keely knew it was a lie, and not the client part either. Dar loved it. In fact, it had been totally planned. She'd shown up at the job shack and threatened to accost her on the spot if she didn't leave work immediately. Keely knew Dar well enough to take her threats seriously.

"I've got a great evening planned for us. I'll pick you up around seven."

"Not tonight, Dar."

"Don't be silly. I've got my friends' cottage. We'll have a little bonfire and walk on the beach. Maybe follow that with some skinny-dipping and then, who knows?"

"I can't tonight. I've got plans."

"Change them."

Keely shook her head.

Darla was taken aback. Keely hadn't said no to her in years. "What's so important you can't miss it?"

"I promised Beth I'd go with her to a party."

"Oh. The girlfriend," Darla smiled. "Well, you'd better have a little nap then, lover. You know how Beth wears you out."

Keely watched her turn to leave, rendered speechless.

"Oh, and one more thing," Darla added for good measure. "Don't forget to wash your face before your little date," she jabbed and darted out the door.

"Hi, Beth! It's good to see you again," Rebecca gushed as she opened the door.

Beth brushed past her, her temper already beginning to soar. Rebecca furrowed her brow when Keely followed her in. Had Beth brought a date or had two guests just arrived at the same time?

"Let me get your coats," she offered and promptly elected herself to help Beth off with hers before turning to face them again.

"This is my friend, Keely," Beth answered her expectant look.

"Oh, hello!" Rebecca beamed, interpreting the term friend literally. "It's so nice to meet you," she shook her hand vigorously.

Beth's eyes pleaded with Keely to do something. She

promptly obliged by slipping her arm around Beth's waist, leaving little to Rebecca's imagination.

"Excuse us," Beth asked and beat it into the living room, leaving a crestfallen Rebecca in their wake.

Having escaped painful encounter number one, Beth checked the room over in search of number two. Louise smiled at first when she spotted her and then, discovering she had brought Keely, shot her a filthy look. Beth turned to see if Keely had seen the expression only to find Keely taking a gander of her own. And it wasn't at Louise. Keely was staring rather fixedly at a remarkably attractive woman Beth guessed to be somewhere in her later thirties or early forties, who rated very probably as the most striking woman she had ever seen. Beth watched the woman as she carried on what appeared to be a deeply engrossing conversation with two other guests. There was something vaguely familiar about her, but Beth couldn't place her and Keely appeared to be having the same sort of difficulty. Either that or she was just mesmerized by her.

"You're finally here," Louise came over to greet them with the ever-present Jane in tow.

"Keely, this is Jane," Beth dispensed with the formalities.

The two parties shook hands dutifully.

"And I think you already know Louise?"

Keely nodded and Louise glowered back at her frostily.

"Keely, why don't you and I go and get everybody a drink?" Jane filled the conversational wasteland.

"There's an idea," Keely concurred and trotted off towards the kitchen, hot on her heels.

"I'm surprised you brought her," Louise started into it the moment they were out of earshot. "Bringing a casual lover to a party isn't your usual style."

"Maybe she's not so casual," Beth followed suit.

"She must be awfully good in bed for you to have kept

her around so long," she observed icily.

"What's the matter, Louise? Jealous?"

"Surely you jest. From what Carolyn tells me, there's ...."

"Louise!" Jane magically reappeared to referee. "Sophie wants to talk to you in the kitchen."

Louise turned her haughty glare from Beth to her beloved.

"Now!" Jane stood her ground firmly.

Louise fired one last dagger at each of them and then stomped off into the penalty box. Jane handed Beth a beer as recompense.

"Sorry about that," she apologized.

Beth stared at the potted palm in total disbelief, but a moment later her gaze drifted past her as Keely and the extremely attractive mystery lady exited through the patio doors.

"Where's Keely?" Jane blundered naïvely.

"It would seem she's found a more stimulating conversationalist," Beth quipped, looking at the two women standing perhaps a little too close together on the balcony. "Do you know her?"

Jane shook her head, sorry she'd ever asked. "Her name is Darla. She's here with Gail. I just met her tonight. She seems quite pleasant."

"And fucking gorgeous too," Beth observed coolly. Keely certainly hadn't wasted any time in cornering the hottest woman in the room. What's-her-name glanced in Beth's direction almost as if on cue and then returned her attention to Keely again. And that's when it hit Beth. The mystery woman and the BIG TOY were one and the same. She couldn't stand to watch any more. She turned her back on them, trying to get a grip on herself and her rampant case of jealousy.

"Beth?" Keely surprised her from behind.

She took a deep breath to compose herself and turned, only to find herself face to face with the enemy.

"I'd like you to meet an old friend of mine," Keely introduced. "Darla Kemper, Beth ... ?"

She wanted to die on the spot. Keely couldn't remember her last name. "Campbell," she filled in the blank.

"Pleased to meet you," the perfectly even, white, white teeth smiled.

"I think I might go and grab a beer," Keely ventured. "Can I get anybody anything?"

"No, thank you," they replied simultaneously.

Keely hesitated for a moment or two and then disappeared, leaving them in an unavoidable conversational situation.

"Keely tells me you're an English professor," the dark hair without a single split-end commented. "Have you been teaching long?"

"Eight years," Beth managed.

"I've always thought that would be a fascinating profession," the brown, brown eyes continued. "But not one I'd be very good at, I'm afraid. I think it takes a very special person to be able to teach. I've always been much better with things than people."

Somehow Beth didn't buy that. The woman could charm a cobra with her smile. She consoled herself with the fantasy that her far-too-tanned-to-be-real companion was really only in her late twenties, aged by endless tanning sessions.

"You teach at Western then, do you?"

Beth nodded. "And what do you do?" she asked like she was supposed to.

"I'm an architect," Darla smiled. "I have my own business."

Beth took a sip of her beer. Not only was the bitch

beautiful, but she was probably loaded too.

"Well, I should go and find Gail," Darla concluded from the distinct chill in the air. "It was nice meeting you."

Beth took another sip of beer and watched her walk away, only to be met with yet another of Louise's hostile glares. She'd had it! She headed into the kitchen in search of Keely.

"Can we go?" she butted into her conversation with Meg.

"Sure," Keely accommodated. She knew Beth had said they'd go late and leave early, but twenty minutes struck her as a little extreme. She wasn't about to argue though. As far as she was concerned, they couldn't get out of hell fast enough.

"Who's Darla to you?"

Keely reached down for the key and turned her truck off. Beth's silence the whole way home was no longer such a mystery.

"She's the other woman you're seeing, isn't she?"

"Did she tell you that?" Keely demanded. She was going to kill Dar! She'd promised she wouldn't.

"No. I figured it out on my own. She is, isn't she?"

Keely nodded. "Are you upset with me for introducing you?"

"Not really. But I would like to know why."

"She wanted to meet you," Keely shrugged. "She was curious."

"So she knows all about me?"

Keely nodded again.

"Why isn't she jealous? You were seeing her first," Beth pointed out.

"It's not like that between us."

"What is it like?"

"I thought you didn't want to know?" Keely reminded her.

"I've changed my mind," Beth decided. "If this is going to work, then I think I need you to be as open with me about Darla as you are with her about me."

Keely was no longer sure it could work.

"So how long have you been involved with her?"

"Since just before we started seeing each other," she replied. "This time," she decided to spill all of the beans. "Dar and I have been involved on and off for a very long time."

"How long is long?" she was almost afraid to ask.

"The first time we met, I was sixteen."

Beth's heart sank. The competition was far, far stiffer than she ever could have imagined. "So she was the first woman you were ever involved with?" she gathered.

Keely shook her head. "I just had a bad case of puppy love for her at that point. We didn't actually get involved until almost ten years later when I walked into what turned out to be her house to do a renovations job."

Sixteen plus ten was twenty six, Beth added. Thirty-five minus twenty-six equalled nine. Her mathematics didn't bode well. Nine years minus at least two with Carolyn still left seven. Her competition was not only stiff, she was also extremely persistent.

Keely shifted uncomfortably in her seat.

"You lived with Darla for seven years then?"

"No," Keely corrected her. "We've never lived together. It feels like I've spent half my adult life splitting up and then getting back together with Dar."

Beth's spirits lifted. All hope was not lost. At least not yet.

"I'm sorry if I hurt or upset you," Keely offered.

Beth smiled. "I'm just a little jealous," she admitted. "I'll get over it."

Keely bit the inside of her lip. So much for keeping things simple.

"Would you like to come in for a drink?"

"Not tonight, Beth."

"I think we need to talk some more," she tried again.

Keely shook her head. She wasn't about to be talked into anything.

"Why, hello there," she answered her 3 a.m. knock. "Aren't we the late-night visitor?"

"I need to talk to you," Keely invited herself in. "I'm upset."

Darla closed the door behind her. "Okay. I'm listening."

"Did I wake you?" Keely finally made note of her bathrobe. "I saw your light on."

"Does it matter?" she smiled evasively. "Now get to it. What's wrong?"

"It's about Beth."

"Oh. Girlfriend trouble," she teased. "Did we have a little fight after the party?"

"No. Not really." Keely paused to collect her thoughts and run her fingers through her hair. "I think Beth loves me," she finally came out with it.

"Oh, poor baby!" Darla smirked. "How awful for you."

"Come on, Dar! I'm being serious."

"I don't know what you want me to say, Keely. I mean, what did you expect?"

"What do you mean?"

"Well, you have been seeing her and sleeping with her for a while now. Did you think she didn't care?"

"Well ... no," she acknowledged.

"I love you and that doesn't seem to bother you in the least."

"Well ... yeah," Keely conceded grudgingly. "But that's different."

"Why?"

Keely shrugged. She really didn't know.

Darla kissed her lightly. "All better now?" she checked.

Keely scowled at her flippancy. Darla put her arms around her and kissed again. Keely gave up. Some things were too big to fight. She slipped her hands inside Dar's robe. Darla gave her a playful swat on the rump and pulled away.

"Run along home now and patch things up with Beth," she dismissed her.

Keely looked at her in total disbelief. "You expect me to leave after a kiss like that?"

"You can't stay, lover."

Keely smiled. "Playing hard to get, are we?"

"You know me better than that," she chuckled softly. "You have to go because there's somebody else here."

Keely glanced in the direction of the partially closed bedroom door. Her arrival hadn't interrupted Dar's sleep, it had interrupted her in the middle of someone. She turned and walked out the door.

"Was that Beth on the phone?"

Louise shook her head and crawled into bed.

"You'd better call her tomorrow," Jane advised. "She seemed pretty mad when she left."

"She'll get over it."

Jane couldn't understand why Louise seemed so hell-bent on antagonizing Beth, but then most of what went on between the two of them defied explanation.

"Maybe you should stop pushing Rebecca so hard," she suggested. "They're never going to hit it off."

"I wouldn't say never," Louise considered. "But you're probably right. Besides, I'm not so worried about that working out any more."

"How come?"

"Because Beth and I had a little chat at lunch last week and I think this thing with Keely is pretty casual. I think she's just playing it up to bug me. I give it until the end of the week, max. And it's not soon enough as far as I'm concerned. Keely is every bit as inappropriate a lover for Beth as she was for Carolyn."

Jane leaned over and turned out the light. "You're entitled to your own opinion, Louise," she conceded. "But don't let it cost you a friend."

Keely lit a cigarette.

"No lover of mine smokes!" Dar's voice echoed in her head.

She poured herself another drink in an attempt to shut her up.

"Drinking won't solve anything!" Carolyn's angry tone reverberated.

Keely downed the contents of her glass, drowning the pair of them out.

Brock walked into the job shack. She didn't look up. She just sat there staring at the newspaper spread out in front of her, smoking. He poured himself a cup of coffee and sat down.

"So how come you're smoking again?"

Keely glared at him and then went back to her reading.

"Darla won't like it," he pointed out.

She glowered at him again but didn't say anything.

"You're in a mood," he observed.

Keely shrugged. "Maybe I've got PMS."

"Don't you mean PDS?" he attempted a tease.

"PDS?"

"Yeah," he smirked. "Post Darla Syndrome. You're always crabby after she keeps you up half the night."

Keely found nothing about his remark the least bit amusing. She wasn't just in a mood, she was toxic.

"So how was your weekend?" he tried again.

"A nightmare," she replied evenly. "How was yours?"

"Great," he grinned.

Keely didn't say anything.

"So what was so terrible about your weekend?" he took his cue.

"Dar was at a party Beth and I went to."

"Ouch," he cringed. "What happened?"

"Oh. Not much. I don't think I want to see either of them any more."

Brock looked at her and waited. That sounded like a lot for not much. Keely put out her cigarette and turned the page. Apparently the topic was closed. He picked up the sports section.

"You know Dar's got to be the most arrogant, self-centred, demanding woman I've ever known," Keely muttered.

Brock smiled to himself. That wasn't exactly a news flash to him.

"I don't know what the hell it is I see in her."

Neither did he.

"But I just keep coming back for more," she shook her head at herself. "Why is that?" she asked. "Do you know?"

"Beats me," he replied. "I've never been able to understand it."

Keely fell silent again and lit another cigarette. Brock

turned his attention to the baseball scores.

"I think I love Beth," she quietly announced.

Brock looked up at her and smiled. It had taken a while, but she'd finally gotten to the heart of the matter.

"I'm pretty sure I scared her off," Beth kicked herself again.

"Did you tell her you love her?"

"No. But I told her I was jealous and that's almost the same thing."

Wally poured them each another cup of tea. He wished there was something he could do to cheer her up.

"She avoided me all day yesterday," she sighed. "And I know she was home."

"That's a good sign," he pointed out. "At least she was alone."

Beth suddenly brightened. He was right.

Keely made her way down the muddy, pot-holed road from the job site to the parking area. It had rained intermittently all day, never hard enough to stop working, but often enough to leave her clothing continually damp and chilly. Somehow the weather seemed fitting to her. The abysmal end to a far less than perfect day after a disastrous weekend. She glanced up from her task of puddle avoidance to see the BIG TOY four-wheeling towards her.

"Hey, baby! Need a lift?" Darla called to her through the passenger window.

Keely just stood in the mud and the rain and looked at her.

"Come on. Get in," Darla encouraged, flashing her best million-dollar smile.

Keely didn't move a muscle.

Darla knew she was in big shit. "I'll make you dinner," she upped the ante. "And then we'll spend a nice quiet evening in front of the fireplace doing absolutely anything you want to," she promised seductively.

Darla no sooner got the words out of her mouth than the skies opened and it started to pour. The gods were in her favour. Keely reluctantly opened the door.

"Wally?"

"What, sweetie?"

"What do you know about Darla?"

He looked up from the tiles on his scrabble rack to smile at her. He knew she'd get over this feeling-sorry-for-herself phase sooner or later.

"You said you know her. What's she like?"

"She's quite a character," he chuckled quietly.

"Come on, Wally," she begged. "I want details."

"Okay, okay," he relented. "But I don't really know her that well. Just from the AIDS committee stuff, and I'm sorry to dishearten you but I've always found her to be quite charming."

Beth sighed in disappointment. That was not the sort of thing she wanted to hear.

"But if you want some gossip," he conspiratorially grinned, "Artie worked with her on the Christmas fund-raiser and he now fondly refers to her as Darla Vader."

"Darla Vader?" Beth giggled. "What brought that one about?"

"Let's just say she doesn't take no for an answer," he snickered.

Beth smiled. So Keely liked aggressive women, did she?

"Checking out the competition, are we?" he gleaned.

"Something like that," she readily agreed.

Keely slowly climbed the flight of stairs to Dar's apartment, lagging well behind her. It was time to wrap up this washed-up relationship once and for all. Keely closed the door at the top of the stairs and turned to face her. She never stood a chance. Darla backed her up against the door and kissed her demandingly, making her intentions abundantly clear.

"Come on, Dar," she whined. "I'm all wet."

"So soon? You know how I like that," she cooed, undoing Keely's buttons one by one.

"And I'm cold," she protested feebly.

"I'll warm you up," she promised as she unbuttoned the last one.

"And I'm tired," Keely weakened as Dar ran her warm gentle hands across her breasts.

Darla flashed her a wicked grin. "Then we'd better get you right into bed, hadn't we?"

Beth looked up from her book at the sound of Keely's footfall on the steps. She drew a deep breath. She'd had to wait a whole day but at long last the opportunity was here. She patiently bided her time and at her cue set out on her mission purposefully. Keely's screen door was open as usual.

"Keely?" she called.

"I'm in the shower."

Beth already knew that. In fact, she'd waited until she could hear the water running. She opened the door and invited herself in.

"I'll be out in a minute," Keely yelled.

Beth smiled and headed into the bathroom. What she had in mind would take far, far longer than that.

"Well, well, well!" Louise exclaimed, brandishing a very self-satisfied grin. "Look who's here. Our dear friend Keely Logan. And check out who she's with. What's her name again? She came with Gail to our party."

"Darla Somethingorother," Jane remembered.

"I wonder if Gail knows she's here? They slept together, you know."

"Gail and Keely?"

"No! Gail and Darla. Last Saturday. Gail told me."

Jane just shrugged. She couldn't care less.

"They seem cosy," Louise continued, once again directing Jane's attention to the dance floor. "Darla's really quite attractive, don't you think?"

"I suppose," Jane responded as indifferently as possible. All she wanted was for Louise to drop the topic.

"I wonder if Beth knows about this?" she pondered.

Jane arched an eyebrow in response but didn't say anything. Louise had that glint in her eye. If Beth didn't know already, she had a pretty good idea she was about to find out.

"I'm going to take a bath," Darla announced. "I'm all hot and sweaty from dancing. Come with me."

"I'm beat," Keely declined. "I'm for bed."

"Okay," she misinterpreted her completely. "You go on ahead. I won't be long."

Keely dumped her clothes on the floor and flopped wearily into bed. It was nearly two in the morning. She'd been up almost twenty hours.

"Don't sleep," Darla nudged her awake. "Play with me!"

Keely forced her eyes open and then immediately closed them again.

"Ah, come on," she whined. "I'll make it worth your while."

Keely sighed. "Dar, I'm too pooped to even pucker, say nothing about play."

Darla screwed up her face. She would have pushed the issue if what Keely was saying wasn't so obviously true. Reluctantly she turned out the light.

"Dar?"

"Uh-huh."

"Who was that woman you were talking to at the bar?"

"I thought you were tired?" she reminded her.

"I am, but I want to know," Keely insisted.

Darla sighed. "She's a friend. Her name is Gail."

"You were at the party with her last week," she stated with certainty.

Darla remained silent. Apparently Keely didn't require her confirmation.

"I take it she was last Saturday night's guest of honour?"

All Darla could do was laugh. She'd known Keely would get around to this sooner or later.

"Would you be serious for a minute?" Keely demanded.

"Okay," she decided to get it over with. "Yes, you're right."

"Do you sleep with many other women?"

"Some," she equivocated. She had absolutely no intention of letting Keely know that last Saturday had been the only time she'd entertained the whim since Keely's reappearance in her life.

"How many others?"

Darla shifted closer to her and began nuzzling her neck. "There's only one you," she attempted to placate.

Keely abruptly pulled away.

Darla sighed in exasperation. "Can we just skip this?"

"Skip what?"

"Skip the fight part and get on with the making up? We're much better at that."

Keely smiled in spite of herself. Dar was right. What was the point of getting into it again?

Darla returned her attention to Keely's neck, tracing a line with her tongue from Keely's ear, down the side of her neck. She then proceeded with intent to Keely's shoulder muscle, chomping down firmly. Very firmly. Perhaps more firmly than she'd intended.

"Jesus, Dar!" Keely recoiled. "What the hell did you do that for?"

"Well, I had to do something to make you at least a little mad," she explained.

"How the hell do you figure that?"

"Otherwise, making up just wouldn't be half as much fun now, would it?"

Keely fell back in defeated resignation. Philosophy à la Dar was something she was just never going to understand.

"Guess who I saw at the bar last night?"

Beth attempted to remain calm and look as disinterested as possible. It was bad enough that Louise dropped in unannounced, as if everything was perfectly normal between them, but she hadn't been in the door ten minutes and already she was looking to stir up trouble. Beth wasn't going to let her get away with it.

"Keely and Darla," she took the wind out of her sails.

Louise nearly fell off her chair. "How did you know?"

Beth shrugged. "Just a wild guess."

Louise didn't know what to make of it all. "I take your

lack of reaction to mean you're no longer seeing Keely?"

"No," she shook her head. "I'm still seeing Keely. I've known all along that they were seeing each other."

"Oh," Louise was taken aback. "Then things are really casual between you and Keely?"

"Not as casual as they were," she prodded her.

"Meaning?" Louise went after the truth, the whole truth and nothing but.

"Meaning, I'm in love with her."

Louise's mouth fell open. "You can't be serious?" she gasped.

Beth just smiled at her.

Louise shook her head. "I give up on you. You and your hopeless attraction to losers. And this time an already-involved loser at that!"

Beth saw red! "Who the hell are you to judge anybody? You're the one that was so desperate not to be alone that you married a tropical plant!"

"A tropical plant?" Louise seethed. "What's that supposed to mean?"

"Do I have to spell it out for you? The woman has zero personality, Louise! All she does is hang around and take up space!"

"At least she's got a brain, Beth, unlike that drunken neanderthal you're seeing!"

Beth bolted out of her chair. "Get the fuck out of here!" she bellowed. "And take your fucking pious attitudes and shove them right up your ass!"

Louise shook her head in disgust. "You're such a lady, Beth."

"And you're such an asshole!"

Louise glared back at Beth's cold stare.

"Get out!" she screamed.

Louise slammed the door so hard the whole house shook.

Darla turned off the lights in her office and went upstairs. It was nearly midnight and she'd worked steadily since Keely had left in the morning. She stopped in the kitchen to brew herself a cup of tea before heading out onto the deck. Heat lightning flashed in the distance. She leaned against the railing and smiled. Poor Keely. She hadn't meant to bite quite so hard. But the tactic had worked. The subject had been dropped in favour of lovemaking, but there was little doubt it would come around to haunt them again. She shook her head and sighed. She'd always sort of figured that somehow or other she and Keely would end up together. But Keely still seemed to want the kind of commitment she felt no more capable of giving now than she had years ago. It felt all too familiar, just another replay. Only this time Keely's quest for more would end with a woman whose name was Beth instead of Carolyn.

Darla closed her eyes. She wished things were different. She wished Keely could understand that it wasn't so much that she wouldn't, as that she couldn't be all that Keely wanted her to be. She'd long ago given up any illusions of Keely turning into something she wasn't. She'd always known Keely loved her, despite the fact that Keely had never been good at the words and knowing it had always been enough for her. She wished Keely could accept her for all her faults and failings too. Most of all she wished she wouldn't have to lose Keely again.

She went back inside, sliding the patio door closed behind her, and prepared for bed. She crawled in between the sheets and smiled. They still smelled of Keely.

"I had it out with Louise this morning," Beth disclosed.

Keely opened her eyes and looked at her.

"I finally got sick and tired of her telling me how to run my life."

Keely rolled onto her back to stare at the ceiling. She felt badly. There was no doubt in her mind she was what they'd fought about.

"I'm sorry," she apologized.

"It's not your fault," Beth reassured her.

Keely looked at her doubtfully. She wasn't convinced.

"Really," Beth insisted. "This has been coming for a long, long time."

Keely turned her attention back to the ceiling. Beth rolled over and snuggled up against her, once again coming face to face with Darla's more-than-a-little love nip. She'd noticed it earlier and had decided not to make a big deal, but now she couldn't help herself. She just had to. She leaned over and pointedly kissed the spot, then watched Keely turn red, bordering on crimson. Beth kissed the bruise again. Keely shifted warily away.

"What's the matter, Keely?" she giggled. "Once bitten, twice shy?"

October

SHE HATED BEING late. She turned the key one more time just to be sure. The car responded with a resounding click. The battery was deader than a door nail. Keely was long gone to work and Wally was probably still asleep. Beth eyed the black jeep parked beside her dubiously and then got out of her car to call a cab.

"Car trouble?" Darla startled her from behind.

Beth nodded. "The battery's dead."

"Have you got cables?"

"It's okay," she politely declined. "I'll just call a cab. I'm running really late."

"I'm not in a rush. Let me drive you."

Beth debated. Things were already weird enough, weren't they?

"I don't bite," Darla assured her.

Beth suppressed a snicker. She'd seen evidence to the contrary.

Darla threw back her head and laughed. "Okay, so I do," she admitted. "But never this early in the day."

Beth smiled. Keely was right. Dar did have an absurd sense of humour.

"Come on," Darla encouraged her again. "Get in."

The moment they hit the streets, Beth knew Keely was right about one other thing too. Darla was a maniac behind the wheel.

"Keely woke up with a cold this morning," Darla told her.

Beth nodded. "I had it last week."

Darla flashed a wicked grin. "I suppose that means I'm next."

Beth smiled again. This wasn't as bad as she'd thought it would be.

"I live just up there," Darla indicated as an intersection flashed by. "But I suppose you already know that?"

Beth nodded.

"You probably know more about me than anybody else does," Darla observed pleasantly. "Next to Keely of course."

"I suppose," Beth agreed. "And vice versa too."

"It's kind of a strange feeling, isn't it?"

Beth laughed. "You've got that one right."

Darla turned onto campus. "Where to?"

"Turn right and then it's the building straight ahead. You can drop me anywhere along here."

Darla turned the corner and pulled up to the front door. "There now. That wasn't so terrible, was it?"

Beth laughed again. "No. Not at all. Thanks a lot, Dar."

"No problem," she smiled.

Beth stood at the curb and watched her drive away. She shook her head. So much for the theory of hating the competition. Things really were getting weirder.

Keely sneezed for what felt like the thousandth time. Her throat was sore, her head was pounding and every joint in her body ached.

"Why don't you knock off early?" Brock suggested.

Keely glanced at her watch and shook her head. "There's no point. I've got to pick Beth up in an hour. She couldn't get her car started this morning so Dar drove her."

"Darla drove her?" he repeated in disbelief.

Keely smiled. Poor Brock. She felt sorry for her brother. He couldn't figure it all out. But then neither could she.

"Hi, Beth. Can I talk to you for a minute?"

Beth looked up from her desk and motioned for her visitor to come in. Her day was getting weirder. Not only had she visited with her lover's other lover but now apparently she was going to have a chat with her ex-lover's tropical plant.

"I wanted to talk to you about Louise," she informed her.

Beth had figured as much. "Did she send you?"

"No," Jane shook her head. "In fact I'd rather she didn't know we ever talked."

Beth sat and waited. She wished Jane would just hurry up and get things over with.

"I know you've never liked me much," Jane acknowledged. "And I also know that you've always tried to stay out of things between Louise and me, and I've always tried to give the two of you the same courtesy, but this time I can't. I just wanted to tell you that I wish you and Louise would find a way to work this out."

"I would have thought you'd be glad to be rid of me and have her all to yourself now," she observed icily.

Jane shook her head again. "Your relationship with Louise, as much as I don't understand it, gives her something I can't give her. The two of you have a lot of history together. I'd hate to see you lose touch with one another."

"She owes me an apology," Beth coolly pointed out.

"Yes, she does," Jane agreed. "But you know as well as I do that's probably never going to happen."

"And she has to stop running my life," she further asserted.

"Don't tell me that," Jane advised. "Tell Louise. I've tried and she just won't listen. It has to come from you. The only way she'll ever change is if you make her."

Beth didn't know what to say.

"Anyway, that's really all I had to say. Thanks for listening," she finished and simply walked out the door.

Beth stared after her in total disbelief. In one short conversation, the tropical plant had defoliated herself very succinctly. Who would have guessed there was a real person lurking behind all those leaves.

"So what do you think I should do?"

Keely sneezed and then sneezed again. She was tired and felt like shit. She wished she knew how to help Beth, but they'd been over and over the Louise thing and she was every bit as confused as Beth was by it.

"Do you think I should call her?"

"I don't know," she wheezed. "I'm not any good at advice on this sort of thing. Why don't you go and talk to Wally about it?"

Beth brightened. "What a good idea. Would that be okay?"

"Sure," Keely sniffled. "I'll probably just sleep all evening anyway."

Beth got up off the waterbed and tucked her in. "You don't have to work tomorrow, do you?"

Keely nodded. "I have to go in. Brock's in a squash tournament."

"Do you have plans with Dar tomorrow night?" she checked the schedule.

Keely exploded with a huge sneeze and blew her nose. "No. She's got some business thing. We're supposed to have brunch on Sunday."

Beth set the alarm and kissed Keely's feverish forehead. She was asleep before Beth set off down the stairs.

"So what do you think?" she asked her sage companion after giving him the rundown.

"I think by the sound of things you should have gone out with Jane all those years ago," he chuckled.

Beth smiled. "You're probably right, except she would have been something like thirteen or fourteen at the time."

Wally laughed with her.

"Do you think I should call Louise?"

He took a moment to consider. "I think you should talk to her," he decided. "But in person. Not on the phone."

Beth sighed. She was afraid of that.

"And on neutral territory," he further stipulated. "Somewhere like the bar maybe?"

"That could be easier said than done. She's married now, you know. Louise doesn't do the bar when she's married."

Wally mulled that one over for a while. "Call Jane," he tossed out. "She'll help."

Beth smiled. Wally to the rescue again!

Darla looked at her watch. It was only ten-thirty and she didn't feel like going home. She toyed momentarily with the idea of stopping by to visit Keely and then thought better of it. She would be with Beth anyway. The nagging suspicion that it was only a matter of time before things were that way permanently reared its ugly head again.

Darla extended her key towards the car door and then stopped. Keely might be busy but there was always somebody she knew at the bar. She turned and walked back up the street.

Keely parked in the driveway beside the white BMW and headed up the side stairs. After her third knock, she began to wonder if the car didn't belong to a client and was just about to descend the stairs to check the office when Darla opened the door. She was wearing her robe and looked like she'd been hit by a truck.

"Well, I guess that answers that," Keely decided.

"Answers what?"

"Never mind!"

"Oh," Darla moaned, putting her hand to her head. "Don't yell."

"A little hung over, are we?"

"More than a little," Darla confirmed, really not looking forward to the upcoming scene. "Are you coming in or what?"

"What about your guest?" Keely glowered.

"I'll get rid of her."

Keely finally entered wearing a full scowl. She was most definitely not amused!

"Why don't you go into the kitchen and put the coffee on while I ... attend to my guest?" Darla finally finished her sentence.

The aforementioned guest opened the bedroom door at that very instant and, while she was dressed, it was apparent she hadn't been for long.

"Keely," Darla started the painful introduction. "This is ... ?" Darla turned to her guest in an attempt at a feeble recovery. "I know it's horribly rude of me," she told her, "but I can't remember your name."

"Her name is Rebecca," Keely filled her in.

"You two know each other?"

Keely shot Darla a look before turning to stride purposefully into the kitchen. She filled the coffee maker, doing her damnedest to ignore the goings-on in the living room. The coffee finished brewing and Keely sat down while Darla still attended to her task of guest disposal. Rebecca was anything but an easy brush-off, and Keely sat silently seething for the forever it took Darla to accomplish her nearly insurmountable task.

Darla detoured by the bathroom to down three much-needed aspirins before facing the music. Keely in no way acknowledged her presence when she entered the room.

"You can yell at me now," she granted her permission.

Keely shook her head. Darla poured a coffee and sat down at the table opposite her and waited. And waited.

"Aren't you going to say anything?" she finally asked.

"What the hell do you expect me to say?" Keely bellowed.

Darla brought her hand to her head. At least she was yelling. That was an improvement.

"You and your goddamned other lovers!" Keely spat. "Why am I not enough for you? Why?"

"Enough?" she repeated. "Keely, you've always been enough for me."

"Yeah. Right!" Keely cut in sarcastically. "Me and a supporting cast of thousands."

"Let me finish!" Darla raised her voice, sending her head into yet another round of pounding. "You've always been enough," she continued more softly. "I just never expected you or anyone else to be my everything."

"So now I expect too much?" Keely roared. She shook her head in disgust. Too much? Not enough? And then of course there was always good old everything. What was the difference? If nothing was ever enough, then how could anything possibly be too much? History did repeat itself. And they all participated in committing the crime; making the same mistakes over and over, engaging in the same conversations, line after line. Guilty as charged. Only the names were changed to protect those determined to remain anything but innocent.

"I love you," Darla offered.

"Yeah? Well sometimes you've sure got a funny way of showing it," she snapped in reply.

"I know you think that," she conceded. "And I'll be the first to admit monogamy's not exactly my middle name, but I do love you," Darla restated adamantly.

Keely searched her face for any hint of insincerity.

"You're the only one I've ever loved," she admitted quietly.

Keely struggled in vain to control her look of shock.

"You didn't know that before, did you?"

Keely shook her head and looked down at her hands. Right now she didn't know much of anything.

"I'm going to go and take a bath," Darla eventually filled the silence. "Then if you'd like, we can fix omelettes or something."

Keely didn't look at her or say a thing. Darla got up from the table and went into the bathroom. She mechanically filled the tub and stepped in. She slid down in the water and listened. The whole house was silent. Keely was gone and it was doubtless this time it would be for good. Her stupidity had cost her dearly, very dearly indeed.

"So how come you didn't say, 'People who live in glass houses shouldn't throw stones'?"

Darla looked up at her and smiled. They were even now. Keely had surprised the hell out of her too.

"So how was your brunch with Dar?"

"Interesting," Keely generally commented. "Actually, I ran into an old friend of yours."

"Oh. Who?"

"Your good buddy Rebecca," Keely smiled.

"Rebecca? God! Where did you run into her?"

"At Dar's."

"I didn't know she knew Dar."

"She doesn't really," Keely grinned. "Let's just say they met at the bar Saturday night."

Beth nearly fell over. "Rebecca and Dar?"

"Don't try to figure it out," Keely chuckled. "Dar can't either."

"Well at least that's a good sign."

"You should have seen the look on Rebecca's face when I walked in," Keely outright laughed. "If looks could kill."

"I'll bet," Beth laughed with her. "Dar's not going to see her again, is she?"

"I think her exact words were 'Not a chance in hell.'"

"Oh sure," Darla pouted. "I get a cold from *your* girlfriend and now you're going to go out with her and leave me all by myself to die."

Keely smiled. She knew what Darla was up to. "You'll live. You don't even have a temperature."

"But my throat really hurts," she whined. "I want some ice cream."

"If I get you the ice cream, then can I go?" Keely attempted the negotiation.

Darla heaved a huge sigh. "What are you two doing tonight anyway?"

"I don't know," Keely shrugged. "We haven't talked about it yet and, unlike you, Beth does ask my opinion."

Darla looked at her, totally stricken, and then of all things burst into tears. Keely sat down on the edge of the bed and took her hand. She felt like a total shit.

"It's okay," Darla sniffled. "You go."

Keely sighed. "I'll call her and tell her I can't come."

Darla blew her nose. "Why don't you invite her over here? We could watch videos or something."

Keely just looked at her.

"Do you want me to call her?"

"She won't come," Keely asserted.

Darla shrugged. "We'll see. What's her number?"

Keely got up off the bed and left the room.

"Okay, I'll look it up then," Darla called after her.

Keely headed down the side stairs to the store. She didn't want to know the outcome. She bought two flavours of ice cream as a peace offering and returned to find Dar sitting up in bed reading.

"You bought me ice cream," she beamed.

Keely nodded.

"What flavours?"

"Strawberry and chocolate chip."

Darla smiled and returned to her reading.

"So what did she say?" Keely braved.

"She said she'll be over in an hour," she wickedly grinned.

Keely sat down on the edge of the bed. Now she really didn't understand.

"I love old movies," Beth sighed.

"Me too," Darla dried her eyes. "Keely hates them."

Beth glanced at Keely, passed out on the far end of the sofa. "She's really tired."

Darla nodded. "I don't know how she's done it this long."

Beth and Darla looked at each other and smiled.

"Keely and I had a big fight on Sunday," Darla broached. "Did she tell you?"

Beth nodded.

"I thought I'd really lost her for good this time," Darla

reflected. "I suppose that wouldn't have exactly disappointed you?"

"Oh, I don't know," Beth hedged. "In a way I can't imagine what Keely would be like without you in her life."

"Well, I remember only too well what life without Keely in it is like for me, and I didn't much care for it," Darla replied. "Keely's really the only person I've ever been close to," she admitted honestly.

Beth nodded. "Wally's really my only friend other than Keely."

"You mean we're not friends?"

Beth smiled at her smile. She didn't know if she was serious or not.

"Your house is great," Beth moved onto firmer territory.

"Thank you," she glowed at the compliment. "It's not really finished yet. I've always wanted to convert the attic level into a master suite. It's really the only thing left to do."

Beth surveyed her surroundings again. The hush the room fell into was broken by Darla's sneeze. Keely stirred on the sofa but didn't wake. Darla sneezed again. Keely rolled onto her side. She was gone for the night.

Darla closed her eyes. Her head was pounding and her nose was on fire from blowing it so often. She blew the poor thing again.

"Keely loves you very much," Beth dropped from out of the blue.

Darla opened her eyes to stare at her, wondering what she was up to.

"Do you love her?"

Darla nodded, even further perplexed.

"So do I."

They sat pensively looking at each other for quite a while.

"Keely feels like she doesn't live anywhere," Beth picked up the conversation again. "She's always either at your place or mine. Did she say anything to you about that?"

Darla nodded in confirmation. "I don't know how to resolve this, do you?"

Beth shook her head. There was no solution. It was like some stupid love triangle in a bad soap opera. As the Lovers Turn. All My Dykes.

"Would you live with Keely if I wasn't in the picture?" Darla asked.

"Probably," she waffled uncertainly.

"But you don't know for sure?"

"Not really," Beth conceded. "I've only lived with someone once before and that was kind of a disaster."

Darla nodded. Keely had mentioned she'd lived with Louise.

"If I weren't in the picture, would you live with her?"

"I don't know," Darla replied with equal candour. "The idea of living with Keely has always scared the hell out of me."

"But part of you would like to?" Beth interpreted.

"Of course," she granted. "But even if I could manage to get my shit together, I always figured there was no way reality could ever measure up to Keely's fantasy. I mean, let's face it. Keely's no better at the traditional monogamous thing than I am. The fact that you even exist proves that, not to mention the tiny detail that she loves you."

Beth fell silent again. They were quite the trio. She shook her head at herself, suddenly afraid she was losing it.

"Beth?" Darla inquired after the strange look on her face. "What are you thinking?"

"Nothing," she dismissed it as an absurdity.

"Come on," she pushed again.

It was totally crazy. Sheer lunacy. Not the sort of thing an otherwise rational and sane person would suggest. Beth took a deep breath and did it anyway.

December

"CAN YOU WORK on Saturday?" Brock inquired.

"This Saturday?"

"Don't tell me," he read between the lines. "You're busy."

"Well. Sort of," she hedged. She'd put it off for as long as she could. "I'm moving."

"Moving? Where?"

"In with Dar."

"You're moving in with Darla?" Brock reacted in disbelief. It didn't make any sense to him. Ten minutes ago she was talking about Beth. "So how's Beth about all of this?"

"Oh. She's fine," Keely smiled.

He'd always known both Darla and his sister were totally bizarre, but he'd always thought Beth was at least quasi-normal. So much for that theory.

"Can't you move on Friday night?" he got back to the problem at hand. "You don't have all that much stuff."

"I don't, but Beth does."

"Beth's moving too?" he tried to make sense of it. "Where's she moving?"

"In with me."

"But I thought you said you were moving in with Darla?"

"I am."

He was a little slow on the uptake but he finally got it. "Oh," was all he could manage in reply.

"The only way we could possibly do it Friday night would be if I could take off a couple of hours early and you could see clear to giving us a hand," she tormented him.

"The three of you are going to live together?" he rechecked the factual information.

"Uh-huh," she smiled.

"And you're moving this weekend?" Brock reconfirmed.

"That's right," she beamed.

"And Beth's going along with this crazy scheme?" he asked incredulously.

"It was Beth's idea."

"Oh," was all he could find to say to that too.

Beth glanced at the clock on the microwave as they unpacked what felt like the thousandth kitchen box. It was five o'clock. Keely would be home soon and there was still one thing that very much needed discussing.

"Do you know what Keely asked me shortly after we first started talking about all of us living together?" she approached the topic casually.

"No, what?"

"She asked me if I thought I'd want to sleep with you."

Darla smiled at her. "She asked me the same question. What did you say?"

"I told her that although I found you attractive, I thought that things would be a lot simpler if that never happened," Beth relayed. "What did you say?"

"Sort of the same thing. But I must admit to going one further," she smirked.

"What did you do?" Beth recognized Dar's bad-child grin.

"I told her that if it did happen and she was a very good girl, then maybe she could watch."

"You didn't!" Beth howled.

"Oh, yes I did!"

Keely walked into the kitchen to find them in the midst of their cackling. "What's so funny?"

"Nothing," Beth struggled to keep a straight face.

"We were just talking about you," Darla answered, with a twinkle in her eye. "And about how much we missed you," she added, shooting Beth a conspiratorial grin.

Beth took a step towards their unsuspecting victim. Darla followed suit.

"We were lonely without you today," Beth closed the gap.

"And we're very glad you're home," Darla sidled up beside her.

Keely looked at Dar and then at Beth and then at Dar again. A smile spread slowly across her face and she exited the kitchen posthaste. Their absurd senses of humour made them a dangerous pair. They were two of a kind, and together they added up to nothing but double trouble.

"So tonight's the big night," Wally mused.

Beth nodded. She was not looking forward to it in the least. She'd finally summoned the courage to call the ex-plant and enlist her help. Jane had been only too willing to oblige. She had promised faithfully to have Louise at the bar by ten.

"It will be fine," he reassured her.

"I don't know," she waffled.

"Well, I do," he asserted.

Beth smiled at him. "You know, Wally, I love you."

He grinned from ear to ear. "I love you too, sweetie."

"And I miss you," she went all sentimental.

He smiled at his best friend. "I've seen you every day since you moved," he pointed out.

She shrugged. Somehow it just wasn't the same.

"And I'm coming over for dinner tomorrow night," he reminded her.

"I know," she sighed.

"And I sold this house yesterday."

Beth looked at him totally dumbfounded.

"I decided it was time I moved on," he explained. "There are so many memories here. Don't get me wrong, most of them are good, but I think it's time I started over. Nicky's been gone a long time. It's time for me to get on with it."

Now Beth was really depressed. She didn't want to lose touch with him. She'd never had a better friend.

"I put an offer in on another house this morning," he went on. "And it's in a very gay neighbourhood, from what I hear."

"Oh?" she brightened her tone for his sake. "Where?"

"Across the street from Dar's," he beamed.

She hesitated on the bottom step. "What if she's not here?"

"She will be," Keely countered.

She started up the stairs and stopped again. "What if she won't talk to me?"

"Then scream at her and leave," Darla advised.

Beth finished climbing the stairs. She was glad to have their moral support but was not entirely certain Keely and Dar's presence was such a hot idea. It would only further fuel Louise's fire.

Jane made eye contact with her the moment she was inside. Beth froze by the bar, unable to move. Keely handed her a beer and Darla nudged her in the appropriate direction. It was now or never. She warily approached her nemesis. Jane smiled at her heroism and politely disappeared.

"Well! If it isn't madame of the interesting living arrangements," Louise greeted her.

Beth sighed. Of course she'd know already. The lesbian jungle drums had probably been beating since before she'd even started packing.

"I'm surprised you'd deign to speak to me now that you're a celebrity. The three of you are just the talk of the town!"

"Louise, don't be an asshole," she tried to head her off at the pass.

"I see stardom hasn't done a thing for your language either," she drily remarked.

"I'm not going to do this," Beth made her position perfectly clear. "I've taken enough of your shit! Now either we talk civilly or we don't talk at all."

Louise paused to regroup. "You really hate me, don't you?"

"No. I don't hate you," she decided, after thinking about it for a while. "Actually, I love you. I just hate some of the things you do. I can't stand the way you continually try and run my life."

"From what I hear, you need all the help you can get," she caustically slapped.

Beth just shook her head at the futility.

"And just how long do you think this little threesome is going to last?"

There was no point in clarifying the situation to Louise. She wouldn't believe her anyway.

"You're going to wake up six months from now all alone and miserable!"

Beth had had it! "Look Louise!" she blew. "I'm not asking you to live my choices. I'm not even asking you to approve of them. All I'm asking is that you accept my right to make them."

For once, Louise found herself at a loss for words.

"You can't live my life for me," Beth seized the golden opportunity. "Sometimes loving someone means standing by them, even when you don't approve."

Louise looked away and then back at Beth again. "You're right," she admitted.

Beth hadn't expected to get this far. She didn't know what to say.

"And I'm sorry," Louise said the unthinkable.

Beth stared at her in total disbelief.

"So where do we go from here?"

Beth had a good long think. "Maybe it's time we stopped being ex-lovers," she realized. "Maybe it's time we got on to being friends."

"Dance with me?" Darla invited her.

Beth twitched nervously at her sense of timing. A touchy-feely, grope-me, squeeze-me tune had just come on.

"Come on," she wickedly grinned. "If everybody's going to talk, let's give them something to talk about."

Beth looked at Keely. All Keely did was laugh. Darla made the decision for her and grabbed her by the hand.

"Will you lead or shall I?" she inquired.

"Whatever?" Beth floundered uncertainly.

"Then you do it," she decided. "It's not usually my job."

Keely watched their performance totally bemused. Dar was in fine form and Beth certainly seemed to be getting into it too. She smiled to herself. One more time she was back at the same old bar again, but for once everything was different. This time she couldn't come up with a single cliché.

The Middle

December 1990

"IS IT THE RIGHT thing to do?" she asked her dear friend. "Is it time for me to go to the mountain again?"

He didn't reply.

Beth reached out and caressed the top of his tombstone. "Oh Wally," she whimpered. "What am I going to do if she dies too? I'm still not used to being without you."

Keely pulled her collar up against the cold as she locked the job shack for the night. She was worn out and chilled to the bone after yet another twelve-hour day. She turned the corner and stopped dead in her tracks. Her truck was not the only vehicle still there. She eyed the car suspiciously as she approached. It wasn't until way too late that she recognized the automobile's lone occupant. She hesitated and then reluctantly got in.

"I was beginning to think I'd missed you," she said.

Keely stared out the windshield. "So what brings you by?"

"I need your help."

Keely looked out the passenger window. These days she couldn't even seem to help herself.

"Dar's got breast cancer," she laid it on the line.

Keely winced.

"It's a fairly large tumour. There really aren't any options other than a mastectomy, and Dar says she'd rather die than lose a breast."

Keely closed her eyes.

"I'm sorry to lay all of this on you," she apologized. "I know you've got problems of your own. It's just that I didn't know who else to turn to."

"She's your lover, Beth," Keely quietly replied. "If you can't convince her, how am I supposed to?"

Beth shook her head. "No, she's not."

Keely looked directly at her for the first time.

"She's not my lover."

"But I thought that once I was gone ...."

"I know that's what you thought," she cut her off.

Keely stared at her incredulously. "But you're still living there."

"That's right," Beth confirmed. "But we're friends, Keely. Not lovers."

Keely turned her attention out the window again.

"Please, Keely?" she out-and-out begged. "I don't want her to just give up and die. I love her, and I think you still do too."

Keely opened the car door.

"Keely?"

"I don't know," she replied.

Darla looked out the living-room window at the house across the street. She'd watched Beth gaze mournfully in the same direction a thousand times over the past year. She wished Wally was here now. Beth really needed him.

She ran her hand absently over her right breast. Cancer? AIDS? What did it matter? The end result was all the same. There was no point in fighting a losing battle.

Beth would just have to accept that. There would be no mastectomy, no chemotherapy, no anything. From here on in, it was all or nothing.

"I went to see Keely today," she divulged quietly.

"And?"

"And I don't know," Beth assessed. "She listened to me, but I don't know if she'll help at all."

Jane couldn't help but wonder if, by involving Keely, Beth hadn't bitten off more than she could chew.

"Keely looks really terrible," Beth worried. "Do you think she's still drinking so heavily?"

"The last thing I heard she'd stopped entirely, but who knows?"

Beth heaved a thunderous sigh.

"I got a Christmas card from Louise and Rebecca today," Jane attempted to amuse.

"And how are the happy couple?" she made herself ask. "All settled in Toronto and living in wedded bliss?"

Jane smiled. "Apparently."

Beth sighed again. Dar had cancer and was going to die. Wally was already dead. Keely was not only long gone as a lover, she was also lost as a friend. Louise's angry prophecy really was coming true. She'd never felt more alone. Jane put her arms around her at the appearance of her tears.

"I'm sorry," she sniffled into her shoulder.

"It's okay," Jane hugged her tight.

Beth held onto her for dear life.

She heard the outer office door open and close. "Hello?" she called to her unexpected visitor.

"Hi," came the quiet reply.

Darla snapped her head around to take a good look. "My god, look what the cat dragged in," she scrambled to recover.

Keely just stood in the doorway and waited.

"So to what do I owe this great honour?" she drily inquired. "Oh, let me guess," she added two and two. "My good friend Beth came to see you."

Keely nodded in confirmation.

"You look like shit," she caustically observed. "Cancer's my excuse, what's yours?"

Keely didn't flinch at the well-placed kick.

"Just came by for one more visit before the old girl pops off?" she jabbed.

Keely shook her head.

"Or maybe you just wanted to make sure I included you in my will?" she stabbed.

Keely took a step towards her.

"Come by for one more fucking over, did you?"

Keely came to within inches of her and shook her head again. "I came by to tell you I don't want you to die," she softly replied.

Darla turned her head, disgusted with herself. She'd done so well up until now. This was not the time to cry.

Keely reached out and touched her cheek. "Dar?" she tried.

Darla looked at her again. Keely put her arms around her and held her while she cried.

"You had no right to get her involved," she vehemently repeated. "Why dig up the past again? Why couldn't you just leave it dead and buried, which, I might point out, is exactly where I'd like to be."

"Bullshit," Beth called her on it. "Admit it. You were glad to see her again."

Darla scowled. "Why don't you just go away?" she growled.

"What? And miss this opportunity for your pleasant company?"

A smirk slowly spread across her face.

"You really can be decidedly unpleasant when you want to be," Beth teased.

"A nasty piece of work," she smiled. "That's me." Darla sighed and closed her eyes.

"Tired?" Beth read the signs.

"Dead tired," she snorted sarcastically.

Beth crossed the room to stand by the edge of the bed. She leaned down and kissed Darla on the forehead. "Get some sleep then, sweet grinch," she advised. "We can't have you kicking the bucket from lack of sleep."

She stopped short when she walked into the coffee shop. Keely was not alone, and the woman she was with didn't exactly look like one of the crew. Beth watched them for a moment or two, trying to decide what to do. Keely's attractive young companion was saying or doing something that made her laugh. Beth smiled at the familiarity of the sound.

"Do you know her?" she asked. "She keeps staring."

Keely turned around and looked. "I'll be back in a minute, Gwen," she excused herself and got up from the table.

"I'm sorry to interrupt," Beth apologized. "One of the guys said you were over here on your break."

Keely nodded. "Is something wrong?"

"Yes and no," Beth hedged. "Dar had a mastectomy

last week. The pathology report on two lymph nodes came back positive."

Keely bit the inside of her lip.

"But her liver and bone scans were fine, so at least the cancer hasn't spread any further."

Keely shifted her weight to her other foot.

"I just thought you'd want to know."

Keely nodded.

"And I wanted to say thank you. I don't know what you said or did, but ... just thank you."

"I'm sure she just realized it was the right thing to do," Keely replied.

Beth smiled at her again.

"Is she out of the hospital?" she inquired.

"She gets out tomorrow, but Dar's pretty adamant about not wanting any visitors," she did the dirty deed.

Keely nodded. She wasn't really surprised.

"Well, I'll let you get back to your friend," Beth decided.

Keely walked her to the door. "Thanks for letting me know," she offered. "I hope everything goes okay."

Beth turned to look at her again.

"Take care of her, Beth."

She nodded and stepped outside into the cold December rain.

She thought long and hard about what to write on the card. To simply put "get well soon" was an absurdity. The florist shop clerk tapped the counter expectantly. Keely scowled at her and returned her attention to the matter at hand. Every trite greeting card she'd ever read came to mind. She finally wrote the same words she'd said when they'd last parted and signed it.

"So how did you sleep your first night home?" Beth inquired pleasantly.

Darla shrugged noncommittally.

"How are you feeling today?"

"I'm sore as hell and I'm cranky and I smell really bad, thank you," came the bitchy and totally honest reply.

"Well the sore and cranky part I'm not sure I can do anything about," Beth admitted her limitations. "But the smell part I can. I'll run you a bath."

"I'm cranky about that too. I don't think I can manage alone."

"Then I'll help you," Beth answered simply.

Darla's gaze held Beth's. That type of physical intimacy was definitely outside the bounds of their relationship.

"Let me help you," she urged her again.

Darla just looked at her.

"I'll just go and start the water," Beth decided. "You come in when you're ready."

Darla remained at the kitchen table to finish her coffee. Beth was apparently going to become the first non-medical person to see what was left of her, and she wasn't sure how she felt about that. There had been many a time when the concept of Beth helping her with a bath would have delighted her, but that was before. Now she wasn't so sure. She downed the rest of her coffee and headed for the bathroom to find Beth sitting on the edge of the tub watching it fill. Beth smiled up at her before reaching down to shut off the water.

"I'm not so sure about this," she muttered.

Beth came discreetly behind her to help her off with her robe. "I know."

"It would have been hard enough before."

"I know that too," Beth confirmed.

Darla stepped tentatively into the tub and eased herself down into the water. She was very busy looking everywhere but at Beth.

"Your arm is very swollen," Beth calmly noted. "It looks really sore."

"It is," Darla affirmed.

Beth went to the edge of the tub and got down on her knees to fill the washcloth she had set out with soap. Her only hope was that her simple act would serve to reassure in the total absence of words.

"So what do you think of the one-tit wonder?" Darla directly, yet teasingly broached.

Beth finished scrubbing her back. "I think she's wonderful," she honestly replied.

Beth rinsed out the washcloth and soaped it once again. She gently lifted Darla's bloated and very tender arm. She washed ever so carefully, terrified of causing any further hurt. After completing the one side, she reached around Darla's back and did the other. The room was filled with an awkward silence as the moment of truth arrived. Darla leaned back in the tub and closed her eyes.

"Am I hurting you?" Beth checked.

Darla shook her head.

Beth knew what she was up to. "It's a very neat incision," she tried.

Her directness worked. Darla joined her in an open examination of the area of her chest that used to be her right breast. Beth dropped the washcloth and ever so gently traced her finger along the line of stitches. Darla watched her hand travel the distance and then risked a glance upwards.

Beth smiled reassuringly at her best friend. "I think it's a very handsome scar."

"So she won't agree to the chemotherapy?" Keely compressed Beth's paragraphs into one sentence.

"That's right," she confirmed.

"But she said she'd do this hormone therapy thing?"

"Yes."

"Is that enough?" she worried.

"I sure as hell hope so," Beth observed. "Because that's all she's willing to do."

"What does her doctor say?"

"Her oncologist — that's the cancer specialist," she wasn't sure she knew, "says he'd like her to have chemotherapy too, but she adamantly refused."

Keely was silent on the other end of the telephone line.

"I don't think even you can convince her this time," she let her off the hook.

Keely didn't reply.

"Keely?"

"Will you call me if anything else comes up?" she opted to let it drop.

"I will," she promised. "And thanks for calling. Have a Merry Christmas, Keely."

"Yeah," she sighed. "You too."

January

"FIFTY-ONE sucks," she announced.

"Oh, come on," Beth cajoled her. "Is that any way to be on your birthday?"

"Some birthday," Darla muttered. "It's not as bad as last year's, but it sure as hell comes close."

Beth nodded in agreement and sat on the edge of the bed. They'd buried Wally a year ago today and then spent the evening toasting his memory and celebrating Dar turning fifty with far too many margaritas. Her hangover had lasted a full two days.

"So what did you do today?"

"Spent the day marking," Beth recounted.

"Still up to your tits, and it is still plural in your case, in exams and term papers?"

Beth smiled and nodded. She was beginning to think she'd never see the top of her desk again.

"I'm sorry playing nursemaid to me created such a mess," she apologized dejectedly.

"So what do you want to do to celebrate your birthday?" Beth refused to let her get into a round of feeling guilty again.

"Slash my wrists? Jump off a tall building in a single bound?" she quipped. "I don't know," she equivocated. "I can't decide."

Beth hated the forlorn look on Darla's face. She wished there was something she could do or say to make her smile again, but she knew better. The bottom line was she was in way over her head.

Keely lit a cigarette. She was annoyed with herself and had been all day. She'd done what Beth had asked her to. It was time to let it go again. She took a deep breath and picked up the phone anyway. Darla answered on the third ring.

"Happy Birthday," Keely wished her.

Darla broke into a great big grin. "Thank you."

Beth smiled. From the look on Dar's face, the identity of the caller was no mystery. Keely had remembered it was her birthday after all.

February

JANE SLIPPED QUIETLY from the bed, doing everything she possibly could to ensure she didn't wake the sleeping woman beside her. She picked up the clothes she'd hurriedly tossed aside the night before and went to the bathroom to dress before tiptoeing down the stairs. She put the coffee on and sat down at the kitchen table, grateful that for once the roommate from hell didn't appear to be awake yet. A round of verbal ping-pong with Darla was not exactly the best way to start any day. It was no secret she was having a tough time of it since her surgery, but even that excuse was wearing thin.

She got up and poured herself a cup of coffee, debating whether or not she should awaken Beth. Jane was pretty sure she taught an early class on Wednesdays. She decided against it. It wasn't as if on those rare occasions when Beth did invite her into her bed she might forget to set her alarm in the throws of passion or anything. No. No matter how much Jane wished things were that way between them, the sad truth was they weren't, and lately even she was beginning to doubt they ever would be.

Jane finished her coffee and slipped quietly out the door.

"So what are you up to today?"

Darla shrugged. She didn't know and she didn't care.

"Are you planning on getting dressed, maybe?"

She shrugged again.

"Have you been doing your exercises?" Beth checked up on her.

"Have you been told to fuck off and mind your own business lately?"

Beth fell silent. Darla calmly got up from the table and left the room.

"Keely! Hi." Her appearance in the office doorway was a pleasant surprise.

Keely stuffed her hands in her pockets and leaned against the door frame. "How is she?" she got right to it.

"Physically, so-so. Mentally, not great."

Keely nodded and stared at her feet.

"She still doesn't have full mobility in her arm," she went on. "And she spends most of her day in bed."

Keely scowled at the wall behind Beth's head.

"She's totally lost her sense of humour, Keely."

Keely looked back at her. If that was the case, then she really was in a bad way.

"I've been thinking of talking to you," Beth admitted. "You helped so much last time. Would you try again?"

She wasn't sure she even could, say nothing about should.

"Please?"

Keely sighed and reluctantly nodded.

"You again," she snarled.

Keely entered the bedroom, undaunted.

"The right one's the fake one in case you're wondering," she growled.

"It looks very natural," Keely trolled for a smile.

"Well, it doesn't feel that way," she refused to comply.

Keely sat down in the chair beside the bed. Dar was making this anything but easy.

"You still look like shit," Darla poked. "And I suppose Beth nagged you into showing up again?" she prodded.

Keely shook her head. "Actually, I went to see her this time. I wanted to know how you were."

"I'm fucking marvellous," she snapped.

Keely ran her fingers through her hair in frustration. Darla spotted it immediately. Keely dropped her hand into her lap self-consciously. Darla reached over and seized it for closer examination.

"I lost it in a stupid accident at work," she uncomfortably explained.

Darla brought the bare reminder of Keely's left index finger to her lips and kissed it. "All better now?" she checked.

Keely damned near fell off her chair.

A smirk spread across Darla's face. "Want to kiss my boo-boo better too?" she inquired wickedly.

"The place looks good," Keely tried to chat idly.

Beth watched her nervously pace about the living room.

"Did you ever finish the upstairs?"

Beth nodded. "Dar decided it should be my room. Would you like to see it?"

Keely shook her head. "Another time maybe."

"Sit down," Beth encouraged her.

Keely flopped wearily on the sofa. She was out of cheery and light for the rest of the night. She hoped Beth didn't expect to be entertained too.

"You made her laugh," Beth congratulated her.

Keely shrugged and distractedly looked around the room.

"Would you like a drink?" Beth offered. "Or a coffee?" she amended hurriedly.

"I quit drinking early last fall, Beth," she put the unspoken to rest. "And I've only had a couple of slips since. I'm an alcoholic," she made herself say.

Her bluntness took all Beth's words away.

"I suppose you probably heard," she went on. "For a while there drunk and disorderly were my middle names."

"I feel badly," Beth expressed.

"And I had a very good time blaming you," Keely smiled sadly. "And of course Dar, that goes without saying, and Brock and Carolyn and my parents and anybody else, dead or alive, who ever had the misfortune of knowing me."

Now Beth really didn't know what to say.

"Dar said your father died," Keely switched topics abruptly. "I'm sorry."

"Last year," she confirmed. "Just after Wally."

"I'm sorry," she repeated.

Beth nodded and an eerie silence enveloped them.

"Did you quit drinking when you lost your finger?"

Keely shook her head and squirmed uncomfortably at both subjects coming up again. "That happened a couple of years ago."

Beth let it drop. There was no point in pushing for something that just wasn't going to happen.

"It wasn't really any one thing," Keely tried to explain. "I just looked in the mirror one day and the person to blame for my problems looked back at me. I guess I finally figured out that nothing would ever change for me until I did," she finished awkwardly.

Beth smiled at her. There was hope after all. Keely was actually taking a stab at verbal intimacy.

Keely got to her feet. "I'd better go," she decided.

Beth followed her to the door. "I've missed you," she said.

Keely shrugged into her coat and reached for the door handle, anxious to be on her way.

"I know it won't be easy," Beth conceded. "But I would very much like for us to be friends."

Keely turned to look at her again and stared into the face of sincerity. Beth was only asking her to do something she both needed and wanted.

"Do you think we can find a way to do that?"

"I don't know, Beth," she cautiously replied. "But I'd like to try."

March

BETH LAY WITH her head on Jane's sweat-dampened chest, listening to her heart rate slow.

"That was very nice," Jane murmured dreamily.

Beth smiled. Very nice was an apt description. There were no disastrous encounters, no crazy surprises, just nice pleasant sex. Jane was every bit as patient, gentle and thoughtful in bed as out. It was very nice indeed. She closed her eyes and drifted on the edge of sleep.

"I wish you didn't have to go home," Jane reflected quietly.

Beth opened her eyes. "I know. Me too. But I don't like to leave Dar alone overnight."

Jane didn't say anything. She just lay there looking totally dejected. Guilt got the better of Beth. She reached over and picked up the phone.

"Have a nice date?" she grumbled.

"Don't be mad, Dar. You said it was okay."

Darla returned her attention to the newspaper and proceeded to ignore her.

"How did you sleep?" Beth grew bored with Dar's silent-treatment routine.

"Fucking awful. How about you?"

Beth sighed. "Are you going to work today?"

Darla shrugged.

"Don't you think it's about time you thought about it at least?"

Darla shot her a look. Beth took her cue and went upstairs to her room. She picked up the telephone. Obviously, her kick in the butt wasn't enough. Once again it was time to call in a bigger shoe.

"Jane and Beth?" Keely reacted in total disbelief. "Since when?"

"It's been going on for quite a while now, although somewhat half-assedly," she qualified.

"Why didn't she tell me?"

"Probably because you don't tell her that sort of thing either, now do you?"

"There's nothing to tell," she defended herself.

"What about that cute young thing you were seeing last December?" Darla tossed out.

"What cute young thing?"

"Sure, Keely," she laughed. "Go ahead. Play innocent with me."

Keely looked at her blankly.

"And if you don't want to talk about her, what about the woman you were picking up pizza with when Beth ran into you the other night?" she cited example number two.

Keely smirked. "You mean Cindy?"

"She said the two of you seemed quite cosy," she nosily poked.

Keely lost it completely over the mental image of new-lywed Brock hearing that his wife was having an affair with his twin sister.

"What is so funny?"

"She's my sister-in-law," she managed to explain and immediately lost it again.

Darla joined in her laughter. That was almost as funny as Beth and Jane.

"What are you working on?"

Keely lit a cigarette. "An estimate."

His ears perked up immediately. "As in a real live paying job?" he checked.

Keely nodded. Brock looked over her shoulder at the plans spread out on the table. They were for a house, and a big one too. His eyes lit up with dollar signs. It was just the sort of job they needed to make it through until summer again. And then he saw the architect's name.

"Where did you get these?" he inquired uneasily.

"Where do you think?" she asked rhetorically.

"Since when are you talking to her again?" his disapproval filled the room.

"Since just before Christmas."

"Why didn't you tell me?"

"Because I didn't want any of your attitude," she snapped back. "I knew you'd climb all over me."

"As well I should," he pointed out. "You told me you never wanted to even hear the woman's name again."

"Yeah? Well, maybe I changed my mind."

"Or somebody changed it for you?" he read the signs. "Just what prompted all of this anyway?"

"Dar getting cancer," her words defused him completely.

April

"GOOD MORNING," Darla nearly sang from over the top of her newspaper.

Beth poured herself a cup of coffee. "You're in awfully good humour," she yawned out. "What are you up to today?"

"I'm going to Keely's job site."

Beth took a sip of her coffee. She counted it to be the second such visit in as many weeks. She wondered what was going on.

"Right after I pick up my new car," she added cheerily.

Beth was suddenly very wide awake. "You bought a new car?"

"Uh-huh," Darla beamed. "A Mercedes."

"A Mercedes?" she repeated in disbelief.

Darla nodded and went back to perusing the paper again. "Stock market's up," she idly chatted.

"Why?"

"Why what?" she asked innocently.

"Why did you buy the car?"

Darla's smile broadened into a full-fledged grin. "Because I always wanted one."

Beth was less than convinced. As far as she was concerned, Dar's purchase was nothing more than an overreaction to the cancer thing. It was an "I'm going to die and you can't take it with you" acquisition, and she didn't like it. Not one little bit.

"You're wrong," she read her mind.

"I don't think so," she countered.

"Okay then," Darla smirked. "You're right. I bought it so I could be buried in it. Who says you can't take it with you?"

Beth shot her a look. Darla ducked behind her paper again.

"So what are these visits with Keely about anyway?"

"Business," she replied. "Strictly business."

"Don't you mean pleasure?" Beth corrected with a tease. "Pleasure with just a little business mixed in?"

Beth waited for her to reply in her usual fashion with some sort of cutting remark, but the witticism didn't come. Beth sat down opposite her at the table and glanced over the front page.

"I thought I saw Jane's car in the driveway again overnight," Darla began her plot of retribution casually.

Beth didn't respond. She just sat back and waited.

"And then I realized that I must be wrong," she carried on. "After all. You do keep repeatedly claiming that the two of you are nothing more than friends."

Beth couldn't help but smile. It was a pretty good shot.

"So she's coming back today?"

Keely nodded in confirmation and lit a cigarette.

"Who is she again?"

"I told you. She's the architect."

"Most people don't kiss someone who's just the architect good-bye," Gwen pointed out.

Keely smiled. "Okay," she confessed. "She's an old friend."

"As in past tense?" she checked.

Keely nodded. She had a pretty good idea what was

coming next. She'd seen the smile that had passed between them when they'd met.

"Would it bother you if I asked her out?"

Keely shook her head at the predictability.

"She asked me out," Darla was all a titter.

"Who?"

"Gwen," she burbled over with delight.

"The Gwen who's working for Keely?" Beth asked in disbelief.

"One and the same," Darla proclaimed. "What should I wear?"

Beth just shrugged. Dar's sudden interest in dating again took her pleasantly by surprise, but she had more than a few misgivings regarding the chosen object of her attention. Gwen was just a kid and, even at the best of times, sleeping with someone half your age generally proved to be a humbling experience.

"We're going to dinner and a movie," Darla filled her in. "Do you think jeans are too casual?"

Beth shook her head in response to both her question and the entire situation. It was clear that no matter what Dar's reasoning, Gwen was going to be the first one she slept with since her mastectomy. Beth had always presumed it would be Keely, and she had a pretty good hunch that she wasn't the only one with that idea.

"Why don't you come over and watch the game tonight?"

Keely shook her head.

"Other plans?"

"Something like that," she muttered.

"A date?" he speculated.

"No, I'm going to an AA meeting."

Brock didn't know what to say. He didn't know she was having trouble again. "Are you okay?"

"Yeah," she responded less than convincingly.

"What's going on?"

She shrugged.

"Has this got something to do with Darla?"

"No," she snapped irritably.

Brock sighed. He knew damned well she was lying.

"Go home to your wife," she dismissed him. "Don't worry."

Brock just shook his head. When it came to the topic of his sister, that was an impossibility.

Darla pressed her sweaty forehead against the steering wheel. Her heart was pounding, and she felt dizzy and faintly nauseous. When she finally managed to straighten up again, she saw Gwen coming towards her across the parking lot. She couldn't face her. Not now. Maybe not ever. She started the car and took off.

She drove a couple of blocks in the light rain before pulling over to the curb. She shut the engine off, leaned back in her seat and closed her eyes to concentrate on breathing deeply and evenly to slow her heart down.

Darla opened her eyes again. It had all started so well. They'd had dinner at a nice cosy little restaurant. The conversation was easy and relaxed. The show was enjoyable, not too crowded and actually funny in all the places it was supposed to be. Even Gwen's invitation in for a night cap was the right balance of laid-back yet genuine. Nothing had felt awkward or out of place or uncomfortable at all, up until the moment Gwen kissed her, that is. When their lips met, she knew she couldn't go through with it. She didn't know how to do it. Any of it. She didn't know how to tell Gwen about her missing breast. She didn't know how to respond to any form of sexual touch. She didn't know how she could take her clothes off in front of a woman at least twenty years her junior. She just plain didn't know how. So she'd run, offering only the words "I can't" in explanation.

Darla watched the raindrops hit the windshield, replaying the scene of her undoing over and over again, a less-than-illustrious end to what was once viewed by many as a brilliant sexual career.

It was 8 a.m. and all was not well as far as Beth was concerned. She unlocked the door and wandered into the kitchen, somewhat surprised to find Dar already sitting at the table.

"I can see by your hour of arrival that your date was better than mine," Darla greeted her wryly.

Beth poured herself a cup of coffee. "Don't count on it," she muttered in reply.

"What happened?"

Beth sank into the chair across from her. "Jane's in love with me," she announced.

"Congratulations," Darla poked. "You finally noticed."

"You knew?"

"You'd have to be blind not to."

"Well, call me blind then," Beth berated herself. Sometimes her own shortsightedness was exasperating.

"Did she tell you?"

"Not in so many words. But she did say she thinks you have a case of it for me too," she relayed. "Do you?"

"Even if I did, I wouldn't be too worried about it if I were you," Darla drily replied. "Not after last night's little fiasco."

"Did Gwen turn out to be a dud?"

"No," Darla smirked. "I did."

"You did? What happened?"

"She kissed me and I freaked and ran away," Darla kept things light.

But Beth saw through the fluffy guise. "Scared?" she guessed.

"More like terrified," Darla corrected.

They both stared silently into their coffee for an inordinate amount of time.

"You never did answer my question," Beth remembered. "Do you have a case of it for me?"

"I've always had it for you," Darla winked. "Right up until the time I went from having a case to being a case, that is."

Beth smiled.

"Besides," Darla went on. "After last night's little performance, the only action my sheets will see from here on in is in the washing machine."

"Come on, Dar. Be serious!"

Darla picked up her coffee and drained the last sip. "I am," she replied evenly. "The one-tit wonder has officially retired," she offered in parting and strode purposefully from the room.

Beth put her elbow on the table and her head in her hand. She had to admit it. Right at the moment, Dar's plan didn't seem half bad.

"Have you ever been in love, Pete?"

"Sure," he grinned. "With your mother."

"Not since then?"

"No. Not really. I guess between raising you and all the hours I put in at work I just never made time for that sort of thing," he rationalized. "You know how us lawyers are," he teased.

Jane smiled and then fell silent again. Peter paused mid-salad-preparation to examine his daughter's face.

"This isn't about me though, is it?" he gathered.

She shook her head.

"Are you trying to tell me something about this woman you've been seeing?"

Jane virtually beamed.

"What's her name again? Beth?"

Jane nodded.

Peter smiled. "So when do I get to meet her?"

"I can't," she declined her offer. "I've got other plans."

Beth eyed Keely suspiciously. It seemed more than a little coincidental that Dar had "other plans" for dinner too.

"I'm sorry, Beth," she apologized. "But I really can't tonight."

"Are you having dinner with Dar?" she asked point-blank.

Keely shook her head. She didn't want to say that her evening's entertainment centred around an AA meeting.

Beth set off to her car totally bummed out. She'd had such a rotten day, and with Dar and Keely both so mysteriously busy there was nobody to bitch to. Beth smiled. That wasn't entirely true.

A block from her destination she saw the flashing lights in her rear-view mirror. She accepted the ticket less than graciously. The visitors' lot was full upon arrival and she ended up parking nearly three blocks away. Then the lobby lizard of a concierge gave her the once-over for the thousandth time before he got around to buzzing up to Ms. Tolliver's abode. By the time the elevator reached the twelfth floor, Beth was long past the boiling point.

"Who does that bastard think he is?" she exploded the moment Jane opened the door. "He's nothing but an old pervert. And your goddamned parking lot is full. I had to leave the car in fucking Outer Mongolia."

"Beth," she tried to warn her.

"And on my way here," she fumed on in, "I got a goddamned ticket for running a stop sign. I mean, Jesus Christ! Everybody else gets off. But me? Oh, no! I have to get stopped by Officer Super Prick himself!"

Jane took a deep breath and closed the door. She couldn't see the look on her guest's face from where she was standing, but she could well imagine.

"This has to be the worst fucking day of my life. First thing this morning I get a fucking flat tire and then I had to waste half of the fucking day sitting around with my thumb jammed up my ass in meetings," she stormed into the living room. "And then my fucking period started ...."
Beth froze mid-rave. She turned white and then beet red.

Jane sighed and proceeded with the inevitable. "Beth Campbell," she bravely introduced. "I'd like you to meet my father, Peter Tolliver."

Keely opened the door even before Darla had mustered the courage to knock.

"Dar," she stammered, in a state of shock.

Darla made a quick appraisal of her attire. "You're on your way out," she realized.

Keely nodded.

"I won't keep you then," she decided.

Keely paused a moment to deliberate. "I'm not going anywhere important. Why don't you come in?"

Darla debated the sincerity of her offer only momentarily.

Keely closed the door behind them.

"I'd offer you a drink but there isn't anything," Keely apologized. "Can I get you a coffee?"

Darla smiled and nodded. Keely disappeared into the kitchen, leaving her alone in the living room. Darla sank onto the sofa and took in her surroundings. She'd never been in Keely's apartment before, and she was taken off guard by its neat and orderly state. Cleaning had never been at the top of Keely's priority list before, but then for all she knew of Keely's life these days it was just possible she didn't have anything better to do.

"So how are you?" Keely joined her.

Old and ugly, she was tempted to reply, but didn't. She just shrugged instead.

Keely sat down beside her. "So what's happening?"

Darla took a deep breath. "Did Gwen talk to you today?"

Keely smiled.

"So you heard about Friday night's misadventures then, did you?"

"Bits and pieces," she confirmed.

"So was Gwen busy trying to figure out what kind of nut case you introduced her to?"

"Not really," Keely provided. "But she was worried about you. She asked me for your phone number."

"You didn't give it to her, did you?" Darla panicked.

"Relax. I wouldn't do that. I told her that I would give you her number and relay the message she'd like you to call her."

Darla accepted the extended piece of paper. "I suppose I should call her," she acknowledged. "I don't want to, but she probably deserves at least some kind of explanation."

Keely nodded in agreement.

"I can't believe what a fuck-up I am," she muttered. "I

take it you heard about my new world's record for the hundred-yard dash when she kissed me?"

Keely nodded again. She didn't have a clue what to say. Eventually she reached over and took Darla's hand because she didn't know what else to do.

Darla brightened momentarily and then went back to looking totally dejected again. She put her head against Keely's shoulder and stared at their intertwined hands. Keely's absent finger made her hand look and feel like a stranger's, just as her AWOL right breast had turned her own body into an unknown entity. She doubted very much she'd ever be able to accept either loss.

"You do adapt," Keely read her mind. "It just takes time."

Darla searched her face.

"In bed and out," she answered the unspoken question.

Darla stared at their hands again. "Was it awful the first time?"

"It wasn't great," Keely admitted. "But in retrospect it was kind of funny, I suppose, in a weird and twisted kind of way. I was having a great deal of difficulty with phantom-finger syndrome at the time," she smiled. "Since then I've become much more ambidextrous."

Darla laughed in spite of herself, which was exactly what Keely hoped she would do. She snuggled in closer, silently willing Keely to put her arm around her. Keely complied immediately. Darla smiled at the instant familiarity. The message came through loud and clear.

"Keely?"

"Uh-huh?"

"Nothing," she reconsidered. Those words, Make love to me, didn't come out. "Just thanks, that's all."

Keely made herself get to her feet. "Coffee?"

"Please," she accepted her offer.

Keely reluctantly headed into the kitchen. Playing stupid was anything but easy.

"I called Gwen. We're going out again," she answered her question. "And where are you off to?"

Beth screwed her face up. "I'm making dinner for Jane tonight."

"Begging and pleading forgiveness for making an ass of ourselves, are we?" she teased.

"Something like that," she agreed. "What about you?" she turned the tables. "Going to follow through?"

Darla smiled evasively. She had absolutely no intention of divulging what she was planning to do.

"Isn't he a fun date?" she laughed.

Keely smiled. Brock was actually snoring.

"We should go out and leave him here," Cindy giggled. "It would serve the old fart right."

Keely chuckled too.

"Men," she shook her head. "Maybe it's time I started taking up with women? What do you think?"

Keely laughed at the absurdity of the idea.

"That's better," Cindy decided. "You were being so quiet."

Keely smiled at her sister-in-law.

"Care to enlighten me as to why?"

"It's a long story," Keely sighed.

"I'm not going anywhere," she coaxed. "And he's certainly down for the count."

Keely looked at her dubiously.

"And I don't have anything against Darla," she perceptively zeroed in on the topic. "I haven't even met her yet."

"Oh. Hello," Darla was taken aback.

"Are you Dar?" he asked.

Darla nodded and resisted her temptation to respond, And just who in the hell are you?

"I'm Theron," he announced, extending his hand. "Theron McFadden."

Darla shook the kid's hand. If her memory served her correctly that was also Gwen's last name. Now she was really confused.

"Hi," Gwen nudged him aside. "Come on in. I'm running a little late," she hurried to explain.

"No rush," Darla maintained her polite little smile.

"I'll get you a drink," Gwen attempted to recover. "I just have to run out for a minute to drop Theron over at his friend's."

"We could do that on the way out to dinner," Darla's manners remained intact.

Gwen silently considered the option. Theron decided it was a done deal. He picked up his gym bag and headed out the door.

"Oh, wow!" he exclaimed the moment he laid eyes on it. "Neat car!"

Gwen shook her head as he clambered into the back seat, thankful that her freedom was only a little over a mile away. An adolescent can ask a lot of questions in the time it takes to drive a mile, and Theron quizzed Darla about her car ever inch of the way. She patiently answered every single inquiry and by the time they arrived, Theron was obviously quite impressed.

"Thanks, Dar," he blathered as he stumbled out. "You sure know a lot about cars for a girl."

Gwen shot him a look.

"Woman, I mean."

Gwen rolled her eyes. He was hopeless.

"It was nice meeting you," he finally found something to appease.

"It was nice meeting you too, Theron," Darla returned pleasantly.

Gwen gave Theron his last-minute instructions as he stood fidgeting in the driveway. She heaved a giant sigh of relief when they were once again on their way.

"Sorry about that," she apologized.

"It's okay," Darla smiled. "He's a cute kid."

"I suppose," she reluctantly agreed. "Mostly he's pretty much a pain in the ass."

"Baby brother?" Darla guessed.

"No," Gwen hesitantly replied. "He's my stepson."

Darla glanced sideways at her. It would appear that Gwen hadn't exactly told all on their first date either.

"He's staying with me for awhile," she elaborated. "His father dumped him with me so he could go off and have the latest in his series of mid-life crises."

Darla took a deep breath at the cue. It was time to put an end to her latest too.

"Dinner won't be ready for a while yet."

Jane smiled up at her. She really didn't mind in the least that she'd been banished from her own kitchen. She had too much work to do. She returned her attention to the open file folder in front of her, but it was no use. She could feel the heat of Beth's body as she stood leaning against the back of her chair. Jane sank back into Beth, giving in to the distraction.

"What are you working on?"

"It's a custody case," Jane half-heartedly explained,

concentrating far more on the feel of Beth's breasts as they pressed against her than on what she was saying. "Lesbian mom. Homophobic dad," she abbreviated. "Another case referred by the local gay group."

Beth dropped her hands to Jane's shoulders. "So it's pro bono?" she surmised.

Jane nodded, melting at the insistence of Beth's hands.

"Do you do many of those?"

"As many as I can," she slurred out, giving up any further illusion of rational speech or thought.

Beth continued on with the shoulder kneading. "Are you still mad at me for what happened with your dad?" she seized the golden opportunity.

Jane slowly shook her head. She couldn't be mad at her right now even if she wanted to be. She wrapped her arms around the back of Beth's neck and pulled her down into an upside-down kiss.

The kiss startled Beth. Even at the awkward angle, there was enough behind it to describe it as almost steamy. Jane let go of her and got up out of her chair to kiss her again. The second one definitely raised the temperature to boiling. Jane's hand moved to the button on Beth's jeans.

"How long until dinner?" she inquired, mid-zipper.

Beth cleared her throat. Jane's timing and directness were more than a little unusual. Before she could answer, Jane's mouth was on hers, once again fanning the hot coals into flames. Beth never did answer. She couldn't remember the question.

"So what now?"

Keely shrugged. "Brock thinks I'm crazy to get mixed up with her again."

"What do you think?"

Keely shrugged again. "Sometimes it feels like an inevitability," she admitted.

Cindy smiled at her habit of viewing everything negatively. "Or just meant to be?" she suggested instead.

Keely caught her drift. "Do you think so?"

"I don't know," Cindy grinned. "The important question here is, do you?"

Darla couldn't tell if she was upset or relieved.

"Is it because of Theron?"

Darla winced. That answered that.

"I should have said something before we ever went out," Gwen pissed and moaned. "Most twenty-four-year-olds aren't stuck with a fourteen-year-old under foot."

Darla struggled not to let the shock register on her face. She had guessed Gwen to be well towards the thirty side of the quarter-century mark. The term paedophile immediately came to mind.

"Or are you seeing someone else?" she leaped to conclusion number two.

"It's neither reason," Darla assured her.

"Then why?"

"There's too big an age difference, for one."

"So you're a little older," Gwen shrugged.

Darla smiled. "I'm not a little older, I'm a lot older. Twenty-seven years, to be exact. Hell," she laughed. "I'm not only old enough to be your mother, I'm old enough to be Theron's grandmother."

Gwen smiled too. It did seem fairly ridiculous.

"Would you have asked me out if you'd known from the beginning about my mastectomy?"

Gwen shifted uncomfortably in her seat.

"I didn't think so," Darla concluded.

"It has nothing to do with a sexual or attractiveness thing," Gwen scrambled to explain. "I just would have been really scared of getting involved with you because of the cancer."

"And so you should be," Darla agreed.

"But I really like you," she protested again.

"And I like you too," Darla assured her. "But I have absolutely no intention of adding an affair with you to my already rather lengthy list of regrets."

"So that's it then."

Darla nodded. The dirty deed was done.

"I guess this is good-bye," Gwen realized.

Darla considered and then reconsidered before revising her preplanned ending for the scene.

She lay in bed, feeling like she'd been hit by a hurricane. And she had. By Hurricane Jane. Beth could hear her in the kitchen. Jane reappeared momentarily, carrying a plate and a mammoth glass of wine. She looked happy as hell and extremely cute dressed in only an old T-shirt.

"Most of it is dead and buried," she elaborated as she crawled back into bed. "Care to have a pick at the salvageable remnants?"

Beth struggled to sit up. Her body felt like rubber. Somewhere over the course of the last hour she'd misplaced her bones. Jane flashed her a decidedly self-satisfied grin.

"No, thank you," Beth shook her head at the offered plate.

"A little wine then?" Jane suggested.

Beth took the liberty of the first sip.

"Is it good?" she inquired.

Beth extended the glass towards her, but Jane leaned forward to run her tongue around Beth's lips instead.

"Very good," Beth finally found her voice to answer.

Jane's smug little grin reappeared again. "So what do you want to do for the rest of the night? I've got an idea or two."

Beth felt like a total shit. She really hated to spoil the moment.

"You're going to go home," she read the tell-tale signs.

"I'm worried about Dar," Beth tried to explain. "She's gone out with Gwen again. I don't want her to be all alone if the whole thing blows up."

"And what about me?" Jane took it personally. "What do I have to do so you won't leave me alone?"

"That's very simple," Beth smiled. "Say you'll come with me."

"I was just about to give up on you."

Keely put out her cigarette and got in the passenger seat. She wondered how long she'd been waiting in the parking lot.

"Let's go out dancing," she proposed.

"What about your date?"

Darla shrugged. "It's over. What do you say? I haven't been dancing in so long. Let's go."

"I don't know, Dar," she hesitated.

"Please?" she whined.

Keely sighed. "I don't want to go to the bar," she came out with it. "I'm having a lot of problems right now with the drinking thing."

"I'm sorry," Darla apologized. "I didn't think."

Keely nodded. "It's okay."

"Invite me in for a coffee then," she decided. "I'll tell you all about my non-date."

Keely smiled. She wasn't so sure that was a good idea either.

"Please, Keely?" she appealed to her. "Right now I just don't want to be alone."

Keely turned to look at her and eventually nodded.

"I was beginning to think you'd broken your golden rule and were going to stay the night," Beth greeted her at the door with a tease.

Darla smiled evasively.

"Four in the morning," she read the signs positively. "Not a record, but from the look on your face I'd say she aimed to please."

Darla chuckled appreciatively.

"Planning a close encounter of the second kind sometime soon, are we?"

Darla laughed and shook her head.

"So, what? Did you bid her a fond and final farewell?" Beth presumed, amused as ever by Dar's love-'em-and-leave-'em approach to life.

"Sort of," she waffled uncertainly. "Actually, I suggested that maybe we could be friends."

May

"OH, WOW!" Theron enthused. "It's a motorcycle."

Gwen looked at Dar, who was beaming proudly. She went into the garage after him.

"It's not just a motorcycle," she explained.

"It's a Harley!" Theron finished, his eyes lighting up. "Whose is it?"

"Mine," Darla smugly grinned.

"Can I sit on it?"

"If you're careful," Darla reluctantly gave in.

He was astride it instantly. "Neat bike," he pronounced. "Let's go for a ride," he eagerly suggested. "Can we?"

Darla shook her head. "I'm sure it won't even start. I haven't ridden it in a long time."

"Too bad," he moaned.

"Maybe I'll take it in for a tune-up one of these days and we can go for a spin."

"Really?" the concept enthralled him. "That would be cool!"

"Now be careful and don't screw around," she instructed him. "Gwen and I are going around back to sit on the deck. I'm trusting you. Okay?"

He nodded. Darla smiled back at him and then led the way up the back stairs.

Gwen gratefully sank into a chair and accepted the cold beer offered. It had been a long day, and with Theron in tow it was probably going to be a long evening too.

"It was really nice of you to invite us over for a barbeque," she thanked her again. "I've missed that, living in an apartment."

Darla smiled and nodded. "We're kind of spoiled here."

"We?" she asked uncertainly.

"Oh, I thought you knew. Beth lives with me."

Gwen raised an eyebrow but didn't say anything.

Darla laughed. "We're friends, Gwen. After Keely moved out, she just stayed on."

"Keely used to live here too?"

Darla laughed again. "I'm sorry. I just assumed you knew."

Gwen shook her head. "Keely doesn't talk a lot. At least not about personal things," she qualified. "So? Tell me."

"The three of us lived together for about six months. Without getting into a lot of detail, let's just say it didn't work out quite the way it was supposed to and Keely left."

"So the three of you were involved?" she tried to sound cool.

"It's not what you're thinking," Darla chuckled. "Beth and I really are just friends. That's all we were ever meant to be."

"But Keely was involved with both of you?" she checked.

Darla nodded.

"So when was this?"

"Keely left about three years ago," she calculated. "But Keely and I go back a long way. We've known each other since almost before you were born."

Gwen smiled at her tease. "I don't really have any long-term connections," she revealed. "Actually, I moved here to get away from them. My family doesn't want to have a thing to do with me since they found out I'm gay. I just wanted to drop out of sight, and I got away with it for a while too.

Right up until the time Theron phoned me and really seriously whined to live with me. His father was trying to dump him with his grandparents again. Theron said he'd rather die."

Darla nodded sympathetically.

"Anyway. Enough about that," Gwen shifted the focus. "So what are you up to for the rest of the long weekend?"

"I guess Keely didn't tell you that either," Darla surmised. "We're going to Jane's father's cottage for the weekend."

"Jane?"

"The woman Beth is seeing."

"We?"

"Beth and Jane and Keely and I. Keely and I aren't going up until tomorrow though. We thought we'd give the lovebirds one evening alone."

"So you and Keely are working on getting back together again?" she presumed.

Darla smiled. The status of their relationship seemed to be everybody's favourite subject of conversation of late. Everybody except Keely.

"Dar said they'd come up in the afternoon," Beth relayed.

Jane nodded and yawned. Dar and Keely weren't exactly her favourite topic at the best of times, but especially not on their only evening alone. Beth had backed her into a corner and she'd ended up inviting them along on what was supposed to have been a romantic weekend. Besides, it had been a long week in more ways than one. She'd worked crazy hours so she could go away and hadn't spent a single night with Beth. She wanted to go to bed on both counts.

"This really is a great cottage," Beth decided that topic was dead.

Jane nodded again.

Beth smiled. "Let's go to bed."

"You're early, that's great."

"Dar came and hauled me out of bed," Keely complained. "And then she set a land speed record getting here."

"Not quite a record," Darla countered. "Actually, I was saving that for the trip home."

Beth looked at the two of them and shook her head. They were in fine form. "Why don't you change and come down to the beach? The water's freezing but the sun's warm. I just came up to get a couple of towels," she explained.

Keely opened the cottage door and disappeared inside, letting the door slam behind.

"She's cranky," Darla illuminated. "I wouldn't let her smoke in my car."

"But you let other people smoke in your car?"

"Other people can if they want, but not Keely," she stood her ground. "If I let her do that, she'll never quit."

Keely opened the cottage door and stormed past them.

"Could you take a towel to Jane?" Beth requested.

Keely turned around and looked at her.

"Please?"

Darla picked up one of the towels and tossed it at her head. Keely glowered back and then stomped off to the beach, muttering to herself and kicking sand. Darla laughed and then sat down on the cottage steps.

"What about you?" Beth checked. "Aren't you going to come in swimming?"

Darla just shook her head.

Beth sat down on the steps beside her. "Come on," she coaxed. "You love to swim."

She firmly shook her head again.

"Dar, everybody here knows and there's nobody else for miles. What's the big deal?"

"My bathing suit looks ridiculous with one tit caved

in," she growled. "And I'm sure as hell not going swimming with the add-on in."

Beth saw her point. "So wear a pair of shorts and a T-shirt," she suggested. "Hell. Swim naked for all anybody here would care."

Darla shot her a "fat chance" look.

"Go on," Beth nudged her. "Go in and change. If you need another T-shirt or something, just go and root around in my bag."

Darla got up and went inside. Beth headed back towards the water to join the others, feeling proud of herself. For once she'd had the last word.

Keely came in from the barbeque to find everyone already sitting around the table.

"It's about goddamned time," Darla greeted her.

Keely glared at her and then took the only vacant chair, setting the platter of meat between them. Darla poked and prodded at the blackened debris cautiously.

"What was this?" she asked.

"Steak," Keely snarled. "I had a little trouble with the barbeque."

"Really?" Darla smirked. "I hadn't noticed. Did you have a little fight with the barbeque sauce too?"

Keely looked down at the splattered front of her shirt. "At least I had the decency to fully dress for dinner," she retaliated. "You seem to be appearing in a little less than your usual attire."

"Well, excuse me!" Darla exploded up from the table. "No one told me this was a formal occasion."

A dumbfounded Keely watched her stomp away. "I was only kidding," she stammered in explanation.

Jane shook her head at Keely's insensitivity. "Well, it was a little hard to tell," she defended Dar's reaction wholeheartedly.

Beth put her head in her hands. It had taken Dar nearly the whole day to get over being self-conscious about not wearing her prosthesis, and with one stupid remark Keely had undone it completely.

"Is this better?" Darla demanded.

Beth looked up and burst into laughter. Darla had changed her shirt and come up with a tie somewhere. And she was standing in the kitchen doorway sporting both, still comfortably sans prosthesis. Keely smiled sheepishly as she once again took her chair.

"Care for a piece of char-broiled remains, my dear?" she graciously offered.

Darla smiled at the extended peace offering and hovered atop it, fork in hand, perusing the contents of the platter indecisively. Beth recognized the glint in her eye, but poor Keely didn't have a clue. Darla's fork caught her unsuspecting victim squarely in the forearm.

Darla closed the bathroom door behind her. She was both upset and at the same time relieved. She'd known from the moment of their arrival that the cottage had only two bedrooms, and she'd thought about how to handle the situation on and off all day. By the time they'd followed a long-since-retired Beth and Jane up from the bonfire, she'd felt completely at ease with Keely. But all of the positive effects of Keely's relentless teasing evaporated when she came face to face with the lone double bed. There was no possible way she could share it, even if it was just to sleep, and Keely knew it too. Unless of course her lightning-fast offer to sleep on the sofa had more to do with a lack of interest than with an abundance of sensitivity. Darla flushed the toilet. Now she was really depressed.

Her bedtime rituals at the sink only served to deepen her case of the pits. Everything took twice as long as it used to. Her body was fast becoming nothing more than a high-maintenance antique. She picked up her washcloth and watched the stranger in the mirror scrub her face. It never ceased to amaze her. She still somehow expected to find the perfectly preserved thirty-five-year-old still in there, not some dilapidated old bag whose mounting replacement parts would soon outnumber her original equipment. First the reading glasses, then the hair dye, followed by the bridgework, with the breast as a grand finale. Aging gracefully was a difficult if not impossible thing. Darla tossed her service equipment into her bag and turned out the light.

She caught Keely dozing on the sofa as she awaited her turn in the bathroom. Darla smiled. Her mental picture of Keely hadn't exactly kept up with the times either. She wasn't twenty-something any more, despite the fact that, to her, she always would be. Keely was almost middle-aged now, a term she'd always hated but found herself using increasingly as the faces of all those around her insisted on marking the passage of time.

"Keely?" she softly called to her.

She slowly opened her eyes and then yawned. She was really tired.

"It's silly for you to sleep out here on that lumpy sofa," Darla decided. "I don't know what the big deal is. We've slept together hundreds of times."

"Are you sure?"

"Positive," she insisted. "Go do your thing in the bathroom and then come on in to bed."

Jane crawled back into bed, shaking her head. The inadvertent discovery she'd made on her trip to the bathroom had only escalated the already bizarre into the totally inconceivable. None of it made any sense. First there was Dar and Keely's all-day mutual abuse routine, and then there was the nightmare of the dinner table scene, followed by their curtain call at the bonfire. They'd hurled every hurtful dagger possible in each other's direction, everything from Keely's reference to Dar as the "Aging Amazon" through to Dar's "Don't point what's left of your finger at me" kick at Keely. And then to end up in bed together? Jane shook her head again. Any understanding of their behaviour, or Beth's apparent amusement with it, was beyond her completely. One thing was for certain, though. She had absolutely no intention of being the one to break the news of their encore performance to Beth.

Darla lay on her side, looking at the moon out the window. She knew Keely was still awake. She could tell by the sound of her breathing. Keely lay two feet away on what had always been her side of the bed. She was on her back with her arms behind her head, staring up at the ceiling.

Darla made the first move by rolling onto her back. She pulled the blankets up to her chin, feeling remarkably self-conscious.

"If my being here is making you really uncomfortable, I can leave," Keely offered into the darkness.

Darla rolled onto her side to face her.

"Dar?"

"Don't be silly. I'm fine," she lied only minimally. "What about you?"

Keely smiled to herself. "It feels a little weird."

"You're wide awake now," Darla observed.

"Uh-huh," Keely confirmed. She rolled onto her side to face her. "What about you?"

Darla smiled at her in the moonlight.

"What?"

"Oh, nothing," she giggled.

"What?" now she really wanted to know.

"Oh," Darla began evasively. "I was just wondering something."

"And what's that?"

"I was just wondering if you were going to kiss me good night."

The thought had occurred to Keely but she'd rapidly dismissed it. When it came to Dar, one kiss almost always led to another, particularly in a bedroom setting.

"Well?"

"I'm not so sure that's a good idea," Keely eventually replied.

"Coward," she declared.

Keely propped herself up on an elbow to get a good look at Darla's face. She wanted to know whether or not she was laughing. Darla rolled onto her back and smiled up at her in the moonlight, clearly amused.

"So you think I'm a coward, do you?" Keely played back.

"Extremely yellow," she specified.

Keely reached out and touched Darla's hair. It was all soft and silky from her swim in the lake.

"It's really nearly all grey now," she responded to the touch. "It's not as soft as it used to be."

Keely smiled at her. "It still feels very soft to me."

Darla reached up and smoothed the hair back from Keely's brow. She had a few grey ones too. Her hair wasn't nearly as blond as in her mental picture but it still felt the same, a little coarse and incredibly familiar. Keely smiled at her again.

"So, coward," Darla challenged her. "Where's my kiss?"

Keely leaned over and brought her lips gently to Darla's, barely brushing them to test the waters. Darla lay perfectly still, patiently waiting.

"That was a pretty piss-poor kiss," she informed her after her five seconds of patience wore thin.

Keely repeated the performance, this time lingering to kiss her tenderly. Darla swallowed and cleared her throat.

"So how was that?" Keely inquired.

"Better," she granted her. "Much, much better," she evaluated it honestly.

Keely rolled over to face away from her again. Darla smiled. There was most definitely an overabundance of interest in the air.

Jane rounded the corner of the cottage sweaty and winded from her morning run.

"I guess I know where you were," Beth startled her.

Jane smiled and checked her pulse rate against her watch. Beth leaned back against the steps to observe her. She looked disgustingly healthy. Jane wiped her forehead on her T-shirt sleeve and sat beside Beth.

"So where are the other two?"

"The house guests from hell have gone for a walk," Jane informed her drily.

"Surely they haven't been at it already this morning?"

"No, not this morning," Jane conceded. "In fact, they almost seemed like normal human beings when we had coffee together."

Beth smiled at her. She knew Jane thought they were crazy. "Don't take them too seriously," she advised. "They just take a little getting used to."

Jane looked at her dubiously.

"Even I have to admit that yesterday's performance was probably the finest I've ever seen, although I'm sure they will find a way to top it before the weekend's through."

Jane jumped to her feet. "I'm going to hit the shower,"

she announced. "Care to join me?"

Beth nodded. "You go ahead. I'll be just a minute."

She spotted them at a distance on the beach. They were walking along arm in arm. And then Darla bumped Keely into the edge of the water and the chase was on. Darla dashed up the dunes with Keely in hot pursuit and then, when it was apparent she was going to be caught, she dashed headlong into the water with Keely right behind her.

Beth went inside to join Jane. She'd seen more than enough to know they were falling in love again.

Jane watched them wander along the water's edge. She saw Keely bend over to pick something up and throw it. She was skipping stones. She lay back down again.

"Six," Beth counted. "Very good."

Keely stuffed her hands back into her pockets and they continued on their way. It felt kind of funny to be alone with Beth. She really didn't know what to say.

"So are you having a good time?"

Keely nodded. "It feels good to get away. And I'm glad to get a chance to know Jane a little better," she pointedly added.

Beth smiled. "And?"

"And she's not what I thought," Keely admitted.

"No, she's not," Beth agreed. "Jane's a funny person," she considered. "She's gentle and thoughtful and all sorts of wonderful things. But she's a virtual workaholic and an out-and-out fitness freak. And she has a horrible case of seriousness."

"Do you love her?" Keely came right out and asked.

Beth squinted out at the lake uncomfortably. "I suppose at some level I do. It's just different."

Keely looked at her.

"Than it was with you," she answered.

Keely nodded.

"It feels like something's missing," she blurted. "But I don't know what it is for sure. Sometimes I think it's passion and sometimes," she smirked, "I think it's just a lack of plain silliness."

"We did have a lot of that," Keely agreed.

"Passion or silliness?" Beth doubled back.

Keely smiled and slipped her arm around her shoulders. "Both," she softly replied.

Beth leaned against her familiarness. "So what about you and Dar?"

Keely smiled. She knew the topic would come up sooner or later.

"Are you two getting serious or just practising being silly again?"

Keely laughed. Jane sat up at the sound and looked in their direction again. She wasn't thrilled by their close proximity to one another. Not at all.

"Keely and I can go tonight if you'd like," Darla read her reaction.

Jane lay back down and rolled onto her stomach. "You don't have to do that," she replied.

"But you'd like us to," she prompted.

"Beth would be disappointed," she neutrally responded.

"Always the diplomat," Darla teased.

"Always the comedian," Jane returned coolly.

Darla raised an eyebrow. "You don't like me much, do you?"

"What's not to like?" she walked the line.

"I suppose I don't really blame you," she conceded. "I wasn't exactly charming last winter. But that's not the problem, is it?" she realized, putting it together for the first time. "There's no reason for you to be jealous, Jane. Beth and I are not lovers and we never will be."

"Not technically," she allowed. "You may not have slept together, but you're lovers in every other way."

Darla sighed. The conversation was going nowhere fast. It was making things worse instead of better, and that was the last thing she'd intended to do.

Jane sat up. "I'm sorry," she apologized. "That was a stupid thing to say."

"I don't know about that," she considered. "At least now I know how you feel."

Jane scanned the beach again. They'd disappeared from sight.

"You love her very much, don't you?"

Jane just looked at her.

"That's what I thought," she concluded. "Then I have a little unsolicited advice for you."

Jane wondered what she was up to.

"Make her laugh," Darla advised. "And try being a little more aggressive too. Beth liked it when you tackled her last time," she wickedly grinned. "Do it again."

Jane stared at her for a moment or two longer and then lay back down on her stomach again.

"I'm not the enemy, Jane."

Jane still wasn't entirely convinced she agreed.

"You're burning," Darla noted. "Do you want me to put some lotion on your back? Or maybe your front?" she braved a tease.

Jane just smiled and shook her head. Darla picked up the sunscreen bottle.

"Friends?" she hoped.

Jane didn't say anything. Darla rubbed the sunscreen in.

"Beth would really like it if you stayed until tomorrow," she tossed out.

Darla put the cap back on the bottle.

"And I would too," Jane finished cautiously.

Keely watched her sit on the edge of the bed. "What's the matter?" she asked.

"My back hurts," she complained. "Sometimes it gets sore when I go without my prosthesis for a while, from walking around all lopsided."

Keely thought long and hard before she made the offer. "Want me to rub it for you?" she took the plunge.

"Would you?"

Keely swallowed and nodded.

"Are you thirty-nine or forty?"

Beth continued her undressing. "Neither. I turned forty-one last February."

"That's right," Jane remembered. "February fourteenth. You went out with Keely and Dar. I was pretty pissed off," she recounted. "Losing out on two counts all in the same day."

Beth looked at her blankly.

"Not getting to spend your birthday or Valentine's Day with you," she further clarified.

Beth's own thoughtlessness over the entire situation struck her for the first time. She should have invited Jane along. She pulled her nightshirt over her head and sat down on the bed beside her.

"I'm sorry," she offered the belated apology. "I don't know why you put up with me."

"I do. It's because I love you." Jane caught the flash of panic that crossed Beth's face. "That and the fact that you don't have a bad body for an old broad," she attempted to cover her faux pas humorously.

"Old broad?" Beth laughed. "Why you rotten little shit," she shoved her playfully.

Jane wrestled her down onto the bed within seconds.

"And a strong rotten little shit at that," she noted.

"I'm sorry," Jane apologized.

Beth put her arms around her to stop the abrupt retreat. "Don't go," she advised with a smile. "I wasn't complaining."

"Thank you for the massage."

Keely rolled onto her stomach. Darla turned out the light.

"Keely?"

"Uh-huh."

"Aren't you going to kiss me good night?"

"No," she flatly refused.

"Why not?"

"Because I'm not," she stood her ground.

Darla cuddled up beside her. Keely scrambled away.

"What's the matter with you?" she feigned innocence.

"Nothing," Keely snapped. "Just stay on your own side of the bed."

Darla smiled. "You're being grumpy."

"I am not," she countered. "I'm just tired."

"And horny," Darla diagnosed. "You're always crabby when you're horny."

Keely didn't grace her with a reply.

"Maybe you should take up jogging?" she suggested.

"Maybe you should shut up and let me get some sleep," she growled.

"Good night, Keely," she giggled at their mutual predicament.

"Good night," she replied.

Darla rolled onto her side to face away from Keely again. She knew she wouldn't sleep. She couldn't. She listened to Keely's breathing. It evened out into the rhythm of sleep. Darla closed her eyes. Being patient wasn't easy, but it was the right thing to do.

June

"So you're going out to dinner with Darla and Beth on Saturday? On *our* birthday?" he fumed.

Keely nodded.

"Figures," he growled and stomped off indignantly.

Keely smiled. Brock would feel awfully foolish later. And he deserved to. Cindy's surprise romantic weekend away would take the wind out of his sails nicely. The only problem now was that she was going to have to put up with him being pissed at her for the rest of the week.

"Thanks for the coffee."

Gwen followed her to the door. "Are you okay?" she checked uncertainly.

Darla didn't pull off her attempted smile very successfully. It was all she could do not to tear up.

"You're not sick again, are you?" she verbalized the nagging suspicion with dread.

"No. At least not that I know of," she hedged. "Tomorrow's my six-month check-up."

Gwen nodded. Both her impromptu visit and strange mood now made total sense. "Is somebody going with you?"

She shook her head.

"I can, if you want me to."

Darla smiled at her. She was a good friend. "No. But thank you."

Gwen fidgeted uncomfortably. "Can I at least give you a hug then? Or would that just make you run out the door again?"

Darla laughed appreciatively at her well-timed tease. It felt very good. And Gwen's arms around her did too. She heaved a deep sigh and put her head on her shoulder.

"It will be okay," Gwen tried to reassure her.

Darla snuggled in closer.

"You'll see," she promised.

Darla gently kissed her on the side of her neck. Gwen turned her head to brush cheeks momentarily and then tentatively kissed her. Darla smiled. Gwen kissed her again, a little more fully this time, and at Darla's receptiveness, parted her lips.

"Gwen, don't," she jerked her head away.

Gwen dropped her hands to her sides instantly. "I'm sorry," she apologized for her stupidity. "I thought you wanted me to."

Darla nodded. "It's okay, Gwen. For a minute there I did too."

"Why are you reading the paper again?"

Jane smiled up at her. "Did you have a nice bath?"

Beth nodded. "What's so interesting?"

"Real estate," Jane grinned.

Beth crawled into bed beside her. "You're not thinking of selling this place, are you?"

Jane grinned again.

"I thought you really liked it here?"

"I do, but I think maybe I'd like to buy something with more room."

"More room?" Beth puzzled. "What on earth for?"

Jane mulled her answer over carefully. There were two

possible answers to that question. She had absolutely no idea how Beth would respond to the words "for you," so she opted for the second truthful one instead.

"On Tuesday!" Beth exploded. "And you waited until today to tell me?"

"I wanted to wait until all the test results were in," she patiently explained.

"But I would have gone with you," Beth protested again.

"I know you would have, but I wanted to go alone."

Beth scowled. "So?" she wanted to know.

"He said I'm tired all the time because I'm working too hard and I should consider myself lucky I've only gained a few pounds."

"So it's good news then?" she eagerly interpreted.

Darla nodded. "Except I'm old and fat and have to keep taking the damned medication."

Beth beamed and then lapsed back into her snit. Now that she knew Dar was okay, she could be pissed off again.

"So what have you been up to?" she swapped the topic.

Beth shrugged. "Not much."

"How's Jane?"

Beth rolled her eyes. "Do you know what she told me last night? She told me she wants to have a baby."

"A baby?" she repeated in disbelief. "As in an infant human that cries and does doo-doo in diapers and things?"

"Hard to believe, isn't it?" Beth agreed. "And we're not talking long-range planning here either. She turns thirty-five this fall and, by the sounds of things, she has every intention of being a mommy by thirty-six."

Darla laughed. "My advice to you is to cut your losses and dump the bitch immediately," she teased.

Beth smiled. The idea had occurred to her too, only a little more seriously. She glanced at her watch and the pained look returned to her face. "I guess I should go," she supposed.

"Dinner with Jane again?" she presumed.

Beth nodded. "I'd phone and cancel so we could celebrate your good check-up but she's invited her father," she guiltily explained.

"That's okay. I thought I might stop over and see Gwen anyway."

Beth reluctantly got to her feet. She wasn't looking forward to the upcoming evening in the least.

"Going to watch our foul language this time, are we?" she needled.

Beth laughed. "Fucking right," she agreed.

"What do you want?"

She smiled pleasantly. "I was looking for Keely."

"She's gone to the lumber yard," he snarled.

"Thank you," she politely overdid it. "How kind of you to suggest I wait."

He turned and walked away.

"It's always a pleasure to see you, Brock," she called after him.

He turned around to fire her one last hostile glare. Darla grinned back at him and leaned against her car to wait. Keely pulled in beside her momentarily.

"What do you want?" she greeted her less than enthusiastically.

"Did you and your brother go to the same charm school or is this just a familial tendency?"

Keely scowled at her smart remark.

"What's the matter with you? Still horny?" she poked.

Brock's hostile look paled by comparison.

"Shall I put this blackness of mood down to something in particular I did or didn't do or is it just due to the state of the universe in general?"

"I'm mad at you," she finally blew.

"Oh, really? I hadn't noticed. Care to enlighten me as to why?"

"I don't like finding out what's going on with you from Gwen," she snapped.

Darla winced. She'd oopsed, and in a major big way too.

"You told her in person last night and you couldn't even be bothered to call me about the good news," she outlined the severity of her hurt feelings.

"I'm sorry," she apologized. "That's what I was coming to do."

Keely looked at her dubiously.

"Actually, that's a lie," she admitted. "I was planning on doing it tonight over dinner."

Keely leaned back against her truck and folded her arms in a huff.

"Honestly," she assured her.

Keely shifted her weight to her other foot. She wanted to, but she wasn't sure she should believe her. Darla smiled and closed the gap between them to inches.

"Will you have dinner with me tonight?" she extended the formal invitation. "To celebrate? Just the two of us?"

Keely's heart rate escalated.

"Please?" she pressed against her.

Keely didn't trust her voice so she just nodded instead.

"I'll pick you up at seven," she proposed. "Okay?"

All Keely could do was nod again.

Darla flashed her a million-dollar grin and sealed the arrangements with a suggestive little kiss. Keely didn't find her voice again until long after Darla had driven away.

Jane looked at the clock on her desk. It was six-thirty and Beth still hadn't called, not that she'd really expected her to. She'd run for the cover of home last night, and Jane didn't really blame her. First the baby announcement, followed by the parental interview. Jane shook her head and packed up her desk, despite the fact she still had hours of work to do. Right at the moment her job was priority number two.

"Wow!" Beth clearly approved.

Darla beamed at the compliment.

"I take it from your attire you have a dinner date?"

"Whatever would give you that idea?"

"And just who is the lucky entrée?"

Darla grinned solicitously.

"Could it be Keely?" she knew damned well it just had to be.

"Maybe," she evaded.

"She doesn't stand a chance," Beth proclaimed.

Darla wasn't so sure. "We'll see."

Beth followed her to the door. "Have a nice time," she wished her.

Darla waved without turning and set out down the stairs.

"And try not to get home too late," she called after her. "Our dinner reservations are for tomorrow night at seven. Try and be home by then."

Darla smiled and allowed herself to momentarily indulge in the fantasy.

"Flowers?" she nearly floored her.

"Sure. Why not?" she grinned.

Beth smiled back at her. She really was extremely sweet. "Have you eaten?" Jane really hoped she wasn't too late. Beth shook her head. "No, not really."

"Then why don't you get changed and I'll take you out? Anywhere you'd like," she enticed.

Beth smiled. Sweet was an understatement. She put the flowers in water and went upstairs to change.

Keely sat opposite her at the table, toying with her coffee cup. Something was up. The kiss this afternoon was her first less-than-subtle clue, and Dar's appearance tonight was number two. She was dressed to kill or get laid or something. And the restaurant she'd chosen was as intimate as it could possibly be. They were even sitting in the smoking section. She smiled. Something was definitely up, and she was pretty sure she was going to like it too.

"I'd like to give you your birthday present now," she announced.

Keely looked around the restaurant. "Here?"

Darla nodded. Now was the hour. "Okay?"

"If you really want to," she shrugged uncomfortably.

Darla paused to collect her thoughts. "I had a hard time deciding what to get you this year," she started.

"Oh you did, did you?"

Darla nodded. "I tried to come up with something that would really surprise you. But I couldn't think of anything."

Keely smiled. She doubted that. Surprise was Dar's middle name.

"So then I tried to figure out something you really wanted, but I drew a blank on that one too. And we all know I never buy anybody anything they need."

Keely chuckled. That was definitely true.

"So being the self-centred individual that I am," she forged ahead, "I decided it was time to eliminate one of my life's biggest regrets and buy you something I should have bought you years ago."

Keely watched her extract the small box from her pocket. Darla's hand shook as she extended it to her. Keely eyed the gift curiously. Whatever was inside was certainly making Dar jumpy.

"Open it," she encouraged.

Keely lifted the lid and understood her jumpiness immediately.

"I know it's terribly late and long past being appropriate," she ran off at the mouth nervously. "But it's something I always wanted to do. It doesn't matter if you never wear it. I just really wanted to give it to you."

Keely stared fixedly at the gift. Darla bit at the end of her fingernail and waited.

"There's an inscription inside," she eventually filled the prolonged silence.

There was no doubt in Keely's mind that the words inscribed inside the wedding ring would match the ones nearly worn off the back of her watch, "Love always, Dar." Keely swallowed and put the lid back on the box.

"Will there be anything else?" the waiter unknowingly interrupted.

"No, thank you," Darla dismissed him. "I think we'll get the rest at home."

"You know what really puzzles me?" she pondered over dessert.

"What's that?"

"Why did she wait until tonight to go after her?"

Jane shrugged.

"Do you think maybe she was waiting until after her check-up?" she speculated.

Jane thought about it for a moment or two. "I guess if I were in her shoes I would, wouldn't you?"

Beth nodded and fell silent again. Jane wasn't entirely certain she liked the look of things. Beth wasn't saying it, but she was upset at the idea of Dar and Keely getting together again, which could only mean one thing. She hadn't just lost ground, she was out of the running completely.

"Tomorrow's Keely's birthday," Beth divulged. "Dar and I are taking her out to dinner."

Jane sighed. It was shades of last February again.

"And I'd really like you to come too."

Darla flashed her a billion-dollar smile. "Aren't you going to invite me in?"

"Was an invitation in the motivation behind the ring?"

Her smile flickered only momentarily. Keely's tone was light, but she knew she wasn't kidding. "Not at all," she assured her. "That's why I gave it to you at the restaurant. I didn't want you to think I was using it to lure you into bed."

Keely looked at her uncertainly.

"Although I must admit I was hoping to get there on my own merits," she winked.

Keely smiled and shook her head.

"Is that a no?" she checked.

Keely's smile broadened into a grin, but she didn't say anything.

"Didn't I just spring for an outrageously expensive dinner?"

"You did," Keely conceded.

"Don't I at least deserve a coffee?"

"All right already," Keely laughed. "Would you like to come in for a coffee?"

Darla reached down and shut off the car. "Thank you," she smugly grinned. "That sounds lovely."

Jane watched her silently brood the whole way home. The evening was obviously not going to end the way she had intended it to. There was no way she was going to get an invitation in. She leaned across the stick shift for her good-night dismissal kiss, only to be surprised by the warm reception offered by Beth's lips.

"We don't have to sit necking in the driveway," Beth grinned. "You could come in."

"You could kiss me if you wanted to."

Keely smiled.

"And do anything else you'd like to."

Keely's grin grew.

"If you can't come up with any ideas, I've got a suggestion or two."

Keely outright laughed. Darla's fear of rejection mounted. She remained paralyzed beside her on the sofa. The next move was Keely's. She didn't have a single ounce of courage left.

Keely's anything-but-tentative kiss answered her panic. She closed her eyes and opened her mouth to Keely's gently probing tongue. There was absolutely nothing to be afraid of. She eased back to get horizontal, her arms encouraging Keely to move with her.

"I'm afraid of hurting you," she hovered uncertainly.

Darla smiled and shook her head. Keely leaned down to swallow her mouth again. Darla ran her hands up and down Keely's spine and moved against her thigh in a slow and deliberate rhythm. Keely buried her face in Darla's neck and freed a hand to caress her breast. A low moan escaped the back of Darla's throat. Keely kissed the soft skin exposed by the two undone buttons that had tantalized her all evening and reached out to undo another. Darla froze. She covered Keely's hand with her own.

"Dar?" she checked.

She took a deep breath.

"Are you okay?"

Darla nodded.

"Too fast?" she guessed.

Darla shook her head and tried really hard to smile.

"Did you want to go to the bedroom?"

"Yes," she said.

Keely eased herself onto her knees again and untangled their legs to get to her feet. "Shall we?" she extended her hand.

Darla sat upright and actually managed to take Keely's hand and stand. She made it as far as the bedroom doorway and then froze again. The moment of truth had arrived. It was time to get naked.

"Dar?" she double-checked.

"Why don't you give me a minute?" She just couldn't face the undressing thing.

Keely hesitated.

"Keely, please?"

She reluctantly let go of her hand.

"Do you want to talk about it?"

"There's nothing to talk about," Beth decreed.

"But you're upset," Jane pointed out.

"No, I'm not," she disagreed. "I've known it was going

to happen ever since that weekend at the cottage. It was just a matter of time."

"Are you okay?"

"I'm fine," she replied and promptly turned out the light to end the discussion for the night.

Jane knew better than to buy that line. Beth was anything but okay. She was hurt and mad and jealous and sad, and now she was softly crying. Jane rolled over and cuddled up behind her.

"For somebody who wants to make love, you sure seem pretty attached to that sheet."

Darla smiled but remained firmly planted on her own side of the bed, separated by the protective layer.

"You've changed your mind," she read the signs.

Darla shook her head.

"But?" Keely prompted.

"But we need to talk about something," she braved.

"Okay."

Keely waited patiently. Darla looked around the dark room. She didn't find the words anywhere.

"Whatever it is, Dar, you can just say it."

"I can't," she shook her head adamantly.

"Oh, no, you don't," Keely intervened. "That line might work on Gwen, but it won't work on me."

Darla laughed. Keely closed the gap between them, but respected her hold on the sheet.

"I wanted to talk about things maybe being different," she blurted. "Now that I'm old and everything," she added pointedly.

Keely looked at her blankly.

"It had sort of started anyway," she floundered about in explanation. "And then the medication finished the job."

Keely had absolutely no idea what she was getting at.

"And I've put on some weight, and sometimes I cry for absolutely no reason. I get hot flashes on and off too."

Keely finally clued in. She was talking about menopause.

"I guess the bottom line is I don't know what to expect," she moped dejectedly.

Keely gently stroked her cheek. "It doesn't matter, Dar. Everything will be fine. You'll see."

Darla looked at her dubiously.

"I love you," she reassured her.

Darla turned her head away. "One of the parts you loved best is gone," she mourned.

"Oh no, it's not," Keely refused to let her take everything so seriously. "We both know I've only ever loved you for your mind."

Darla's upset gave way to outright laughter again. Keely promptly seized the opportunity and pulled the sheet from between them to at long last press the full length of their nakedness together.

"You can't back out now," she pointed out as she further improved her positioning. "You're not going anywhere until you finish what you started."

Darla looked up at her and smiled. "No, I suppose not," she agreed. "Especially not now that you're on top of me."

Keely lowered her mouth to give Dar's upper lip and then her lower one a nibble. Darla smiled. Keely kissed her tenderly. Darla's hands travelled down her back to cup her ass. Their mouths met hungrily. Darla's arms and legs wrapped around her, bringing their skin on skin contact to an absolute maximum. Keely's lips travelled to her throat and neck. Darla closed her eyes and swallowed as she shifted lower on the bed. She shivered as Keely's teeth and tongue caressed her already erect nipple. Keely ran her hand up the inside of her thigh and leaned over to gently brush her lips along the scar that had taken the other breast's place. Darla stiffened abruptly. She buried her hands in Keely's hair, anxious for her not to linger there. She shuddered as Keely's hand skimmed her pubic hair.

"Just relax," Keely encouraged her.

"Easy for you to say," she twitched uncomfortably. "You're not the one living in a stranger's body that has only one tit and may or may not do what you want it to."

Keely dipped into her sticky wetness. "It will do what we want it to," she smiled.

The ever-so-slow strokes of Keely's fingers made Darla view it as a viable option for the first time.

"I've been wanting to do this for a very long time," Keely admitted.

Darla nodded but didn't say anything. In fact, she wasn't making any sound at all. Keely didn't know what to make of it. Silent passiveness was not exactly Dar's usual bed-room style. She trolled for a reaction by taking her swollen hardness between her finger and thumb. Her legs opened marginally wider. Keely rimmed her vaginal opening with the stump of her finger. Her hips raised off the bed to meet her. She returned her mouth to engulf Darla's once again and groaned as Darla's hand met hers to guide her inside.

"Is that what you want?" she asked as she slipped first one and then two fingers in.

Darla moaned barely audibly in confirmation. Keely pressed deep inside her while circling with her thumb.

"And that?" she checked.

Darla grasped her forearm as a yes.

Keely covered Darla's mouth with her own once more and moved as her lover's body asked her to. She plunged her tongue deep into her mouth and Darla sucked it greedily.

Suddenly her mouth went slack and she arched her back.

"Fucking shit!!" she exploded loudly into orgasm.

Keely fell back on the bed in a fit of laughter. Her lover, her vocal Dar, was at long last resoundingly back.

"I'm sorry," she apologized.

"Don't be silly," Jane dismissed the entire thing.

Beth put her arms around her. "What would I do without you?"

Jane tentatively kissed her to test the waters again.

"Good night," Beth dismissed even the remote possibility and promptly rolled over for the night.

Keely finally mustered the strength to roll from between Darla's thighs, only to collapse on the bed beside her. Her entire body ached and her knees and elbows were chafed. She couldn't remember ever feeling so wonderful. She reached up to wipe her chin with the heel of her hand, then attempted to extract an errant pubic hair. Darla curled down around her and playfully mopped her face with the sheet.

"You always were a messy eater," she teased.

Keely grinned inanely. Her face hurt like hell. She'd probably have a rash for days.

Darla kissed her on top of the head and smiled. Her hair was sticky too. "Do you want me to make love to you again?"

Keely laughed and shook her head. Yet another orgasm was simply out of the question. She groaned and heaved herself upright to sit on the edge of the bed.

"Where are you going?"

"To the bathroom. Okay?"

Darla sighed contentedly. The birds were starting up. It was nearly morning. She heard the toilet flush and then the sound of Keely in the kitchen. Her stomach growled. She was hungry too. She got out of bed, slipped on Keely's shirt and went to find out what was on the menu. She arrived to find Keely leaning on the kitchen counter, smoking and staring fixedly at her birthday gift.

"Ah. So that explains it. You came out to sneak a cigarette!"

"You wouldn't let me have one in bed, now would you?" she countered.

"Damned right! One of us with cancer is more than enough, if you ask me."

Keely went back to staring at the ring again. The last thing she wanted to do was argue.

"Still trying to figure out what it means?"

"I don't know," she shrugged. "Should I be?"

Darla opened the nearest kitchen cupboard. "Do you have any cookies?"

Keely retrieved them from the cupboard below.

"Chocolate chip," her eyes lit up and she snatched them.

Keely took another drag off her cigarette.

"I meant what I said at the restaurant," she mumbled as she munched. "All of it. Don't feel like you have to wear it."

"But what if I want to?" she cautiously broached.

Darla smiled. "That would make me very happy."

Keely held her gaze momentarily, picked up the ring and put it on. She was surprised. It fit perfectly.

"I love you," she said.

Keely looked up at her. "And I love you too," she got all choked up.

"Enough to let me eat cookies in your bed?" she couldn't

handle tears at five in the morning.

Keely smiled at her. "Enough to put up with just about anything from you."

Jane rubbed her lips gently across the nape of her neck.

"Don't," Beth grumped.

Jane rolled onto her back. That was two no's in a row, both last night and this morning. Now she was crabby too.

"I want to go back to sleep," she muttered. "Stop tossing and turning so much."

Jane made a face at the ceiling.

"Why don't you just get up instead of lying there all pissed off at me?"

She didn't have to be asked twice. She promptly got out of bed.

Darla eased out from under her arm cautiously. Keely stirred but didn't awaken.

"Happy Birthday," Darla whispered and gently kissed her.

Keely smiled back at her in her sleep. Darla got as far as the end of the bed on her mission and then retreated to slip into Keely's shirt, too self-conscious to chance getting caught naked in the light of day.

She washed her hands before taking the liberty of helping herself to Keely's toothbrush. When she looked in the mirror, she nearly dropped it in shock. The woman she saw foaming at the mouth was neither the old bag she was struggling to accept nor the thirty-five-year-old fantasy. She was somewhere in between, forty-five or so, she estimated generously. Darla rinsed her mouth and then grinned at her own reflection. Being crazy in love definitely seemed to agree.

"She always gets everything," Beth announced with a pout.

Jane just looked at her. She was tired of listening. Last night's tears beat the hell out of today's "I hate Dar" diatribe. All Jane wanted to do was get away. She wanted to go for a run.

"Personally, I think the woman's got horseshoes rammed up her ass," Beth decided. "First she gets the damned car and now she's got Keely."

"All of that and cancer too," Jane retaliated in frustration. "You're right, Beth. She's got the car of your dreams and the woman of your dreams and she's only down one breast."

Beth's mouth dropped open. Jane wasn't saying another thing.

"Shit!" Beth swore at herself.

Jane smiled. Now that was better.

"I'm being an asshole."

Jane nodded. It was time to grow up.

"What am I going to do?"

Jane shrugged. "That's up to you."

Beth chewed on the inside of her lip. She had some heavy-duty thinking to do.

"I'm going for a run," Jane announced.

"I wouldn't blame you if you didn't come back," Beth muttered.

Jane smiled. The danger of that had passed right about the time Beth stopped doing her dangerously fine impersonation of Louise.

"Where are we going?"

Darla glanced down at the hand-drawn map and then

whipped around the corner at the last possible second. "It's a surprise," she sidestepped.

Keely was less than impressed. She'd already had more than enough "surprises" for one day and most of them weren't exactly pleasant either. She'd hoped to spend her birthday with Dar in bed but was suffering through a bad rerun instead. She'd been ordered around right from the moment she opened her eyes to find Dar already showered and fully dressed, and now she was having to suffer through another car ride, on gravel roads no less. Keely closed her eyes to the blur of scenery passing by and then snapped them open again as her shoulder strap locked into position for the impending collision. Her arm shot involuntarily to the dash and remained there long after Darla had stopped the Mercedes. There was no crash. Apparently they had just reached their destination, which as near as Keely could tell was absolutely nowhere. Darla grinned at her sheepishly as Keely inspected the damage. She'd ripped the armpit out of her shirt.

"Hallelujah," Darla laughed. "It's finally dead. Can I bury it?"

Keely ignored her completely.

"Come on, Keely," she coaxed. "The poor old thing was bound to kick off sooner or later. It's ancient. Pre-Carolyn even."

Keely shot her a look but didn't say anything.

"Your wardrobe could use some serious updating anyway," she opted for some levity.

"Well, excuse me," Keely growled. "But my fashion consultant wasn't around for a few years."

"And whose fault was that?" she quipped back. "You're the one who fired me."

Keely opened the car door. "And you're the one who really fucked me over by sleeping with Beth!"

Darla put her head in her hands at the door slam. The inevitable had happened. The past had reappeared in the present to take away all hope of any future together.

"I was beginning to think you weren't going to come looking for me."

Jane smiled at her naked lover as she lay on the bed.

"Are you going to stand there grinning all day or do you think you might join me?"

"I'm all hot and sweaty from being outside," she warned. "And I haven't taken a shower since I went for my run."

"How awful," Beth beamed.

Jane made a head-long dive into the waterbed.

Darla took a deep breath and started the long slow walk to join her. Keely didn't even acknowledge her arrival. She just leaned against the fence post, silently smoking.

"Over our temper tantrum yet?" she tried light and fluffy.

"Fuck you!"

"Okay," she easily agreed. "On the grass or in the car?"

"You pick," Keely snapped. "You're the expert on the topic."

Darla sighed. "I love you."

"Big fucking deal!" she blew. "That's what you said last time and the time before. Hell," she laughed. "You'll probably say the same thing next time too."

"There isn't going to be a next time."

"Sure," she snorted. "There wasn't going to be a next time last time either. Remember? You were never going to sleep with Beth."

"It only happened the one time," she tried to explain.

"Only because you got caught," she cut her off. "So what's next? Going home to sleep with her again now that you're back into the swing of things? It should be very appealing to both of you this time," she caustically spat. "You can fuck Jane and me over simultaneously!"

"I said it to you then and I'll say it to you again. Beth was not to blame."

"She certainly didn't seem to be objecting to your head being stuffed between her legs when I walked in!" Keely recounted bitterly.

Darla cringed at the vividness of the memory. Such stupidity! "It was my fault, Keely," she maintained. "Beth never would have initiated anything."

"So I suppose that means it's her turn this time then?" Keely jabbed sarcastically.

Darla took a deep breath in an attempt to remain rational and sane. "There really isn't going to be a next time," she promised again. "Not with Beth. Not with anyone."

Keely shook her head in disgust. "I don't believe you."

"I know you don't," she conceded. "But it's true. Getting cancer made me realize that right now may be the only someday I've got left to commit to you."

Keely's face softened marginally.

"When you came and told me last December that you'd always love me, I realized that your loving me is the only worthwhile thing that's ever happened to me," she seized the opportunity. "That's what made me decide to have the surgery. I wanted more time with you."

"Come on, Dar," she called her on it. "Surely you can do better than that. What about your attempted foray with Gwen?"

Darla looked down at her feet. "That was the last step in the process," she answered softly. "The night I came to talk to you about Gwen I realized that maybe it wasn't too late for us as lovers after all. The way you were with me made me see that even though I didn't deserve it, you loved me enough to give me another chance."

Keely winced at the accuracy of her statement and gazed off in the distance.

"I'm sorry, Keely," she quietly offered. "For everything. I wish I could go back and do it all over again."

Keely sighed. If wishes were horses, then beggars would ride. She looked back at her when she realized she was crying.

"I don't know why we always have to argue on your birthday," she blubbered.

Keely shook her head and ran her fingers through her hair. She wasn't going to get into magical thinking again. The past was gone and it was time to leave it behind them. "So what are we doing here anyway?" she stepped firmly back into the present.

"Looking at a lot," she sniffled.

"Any particular reason?" Keely inquired.

"It's for me. For my retirement house. The one I was hoping you'd build for me next summer."

Keely took her hand. "Come on then, Old Girl. Take me for a walk and show me the survey markers."

The phone's insistent ringing brought Jane out of her sex-induced dreamland. She could hear Beth talking to someone but was still too dozy to follow what she was saying.

"Jane," Beth gently rubbed her back. "We have to get up now. We're already an hour late."

"What time is it?" she yawned.

"It's after seven."

"After seven? Who called?"

"The restaurant," Beth filled her in while making her way to the bathroom. "They wanted to know whether or not to hold the reservation."

"What did you tell them?"

"I asked them to move it until nine," Beth relayed. "I wonder where the hell Keely and Dar are? I hope nothing's wrong."

Jane wasn't about to suggest that perhaps they too were indulging in a post-orgasmic nap.

"Can you try calling them at Keely's? And if they're not there then try them on the car phone?"

"Sure," Jane agreed. "Where are the numbers?"

"In the book by the phone. Thanks, hon."

Jane smiled, totally elated. Beth had actually used a term of endearment. She picked up the phone and tried Keely's. She gave up after a full five rings and tried the car phone instead. For some reason the line never connected so she entered the numbers again. Finally the electronic ringer warbled.

It startled Keely so badly she literally jumped and banged her head. "What the hell is that?"

Darla struggled to squirm out from under her. "The car phone," she muttered, wondering why she'd ever installed the obnoxious thing. "Your knee is on my pants," she finally identified the source of her difficulties.

"Sorry," she chuckled and dutifully lifted her leg.

Darla reefed up her pants and reached over the back of the front seat to grab it on the third ring.

"Hi, Dar. It's Jane. Is everything okay? It's after seven. We were starting to get worried."

Darla checked her watch in confirmation and watched Keely tuck her shirt back in. "Everything's fine," she replied. "A little something came up and it's taken us longer than we anticipated."

Keely broke into howls of laughter.

"We'll be about another hour," she estimated, with a straight face. "See you then."

"We're not an hour outside town," Keely pointed out.

Darla leaned into the front seat to hang up the phone. "I know that," she grinned, once again undoing Keely's buttons one by one. "Now where were we?"

She wasn't prepared for the sneak attack. They didn't come in the front door; they came up the back stairs, joining them on the deck. The moment Beth laid eyes on them she knew it wasn't going to be easy. There was a glow about the pair of them, and Dar looked positively radioactive.

Jane saw the look spreading over Beth's face. "Happy Birthday, Keely," she said, to fill the blank air space.

Beth looked up from her plate to watch Keely attempting some serious conversation with Jane and then took a good long look at Keely's new ring again. Keely twitched notice-ably under her scrutiny. Beth smiled at her.

"That's a very unusual sunburn," she just couldn't resist.

Keely smiled.

"However did you get it just around your mouth like that?" she asked innocently.

Keely's grin grew and Darla laughed. Jane smiled at Beth's bizarre way of dealing with things.

"A little too much southern exposure?" Beth speculated wickedly.

All three of her dinner companions lost it completely.

"Thank you," she kissed Beth, then Jane, and sat back down to glare in Darla's direction again.

Darla held up her hands in innocence. "I didn't do it," she refused to accept any responsibility. "Tell her, Beth," she pleaded.

"Do what?" Beth inquired.

"I didn't suggest to you that you buy her clothes, right?"

Beth looked from Darla back to Keely again. "Am I missing something?"

Keely smiled at Darla knowingly. "Not really."

Jane caught a glimpse of the heat that passed between them. "Maybe it's time I headed for home," she decided.

Beth shot her a pleading look.

"Are you still planning on coming with me?" she tactfully responded.

Beth was on her feet immediately.

"Do you have any idea of how much I love you?"

Keely smiled. "Enough to let me turn the lights on?"

Darla nuzzled her neck and teased her ear with her tongue as diversion tactic number one.

"This is really silly, Dar. You insisted I turn out the lights last night and you wouldn't even let me undo one measly button in the car."

Darla shifted lower on the bed.

"I don't intend to continue to make love in the dark or with you half dressed."

Darla's lips brushed her nipple.

"Are you listening to me?"

Darla's hand silenced her completely.

"There's nothing wrong with the dark," the slow deep strokes of her finger insisted.

Keely closed her eyes.

"Is there?" her hot breath singed Keely's thigh.

"Mmm," Keely approved of her tongue's coercion tactics wholeheartedly.

Darla paused momentarily. "Do you love me?"

"More than anything," Keely replied, melting into her mouth unconditionally. Her silent passiveness had passed and her excessive modesty would too. Like all other things between them, it would find its own time.

Jane watched her sipping a Scotch from the vantage point of her favourite chair. She hadn't said two words since they'd arrived. "What's going on in there?"

"I was just thinking about you," Beth answered honestly.

Jane waited.

"I was thinking about how remarkably patient and considerate you are," she further expanded.

Jane looked at her, genuinely perplexed. If she didn't know better, she'd think she was serious.

"You're a very special person," she told her Jane. "I don't know how I would have made it through today without you."

Jane didn't know what to say.

"Have I told you lately that I love you?" the words almost easily slipped out.

Darla opened one eye and smiled at her from her position on the lounge chair. "You're home," she stated the obvious.

Beth nodded and sat down to catch some sun. "Jane had to go into work. Where's Keely?"

"She's gone to her brother's for dinner. I'm sure in a little while we'll be able to hear the yelling even from here," she grinned devilishly. "I can only imagine what pearls of wisdom he'll have to offer on the topic of the ring."

Beth smiled but didn't say anything.

"And what about you?" she checked uncertainly.

Beth shrugged evasively.

Darla sat upright in her chair. "Are you upset?"

"That phase has pretty much passed," she laughed. "Jane put a pretty firm end to my feeling sorry for myself yesterday."

Darla smiled uneasily. Her blithe reaction was a little hard to read.

"I'll get over it," she assured her. "There's no need for you to feel guilty that you're so happy. You are happy, aren't you?"

Darla nodded.

"Good," Beth approved. "Then I'm happy for you."

Darla looked at her for a moment or two and then lay back down in her chair.

"Did you and Keely talk about what happened with us?" she asked her out of nowhere.

Darla sat up again.

"Did you?"

"We fought about it yesterday and finally managed to talk about it today," she relayed.

Beth nodded but didn't say anything.

"Did you ever tell Jane?"

"Nooo!" she adamantly dismissed even the remote possibility. "Jane would never understand. She's not exactly the type of person that sort of shit happens to."

"No, I suppose not," Darla couldn't disagree.

"Does Keely? Understand, I mean?"

"I think so. She asked a lot of questions about how you and I resolved things."

"Do you think I should talk to her about it too?"

"I don't think she feels like she needs to."

Beth bit the inside of her lip pensively.

"But maybe you need to?" Darla guessed.

She shook her head.

"What is it then?"

Beth fidgeted uncomfortably. "I guess I was just wondering if you still think we made the right decision?" she divulged hesitantly. "Do you still believe our choice to be long-term friends instead of probably just short-term lovers was for the best?"

"I do," she answered in all honesty. "What about you?"

Beth smiled at her best friend. She did too. "So how did everything go?" she really wanted to know.

Darla smiled. She knew exactly what she was getting at. "There is sex after menopause," she confirmed with a smirk.

"So she's still as good in bed then?" she teased.

Darla shook her head.

"She's not?" Beth reacted in disbelief.

She shook her head to torment her again.

"Oh," Beth didn't know what else to say.

"She's better," Darla grinned wickedly.

July

"SO WHAT ARE the two of you up to tonight?"

"Dar's coming over for dinner and then we'll probably just sit around and talk," Gwen relayed.

Keely nodded but didn't say anything. It didn't take a genius to figure out she was definitely not amused.

"If that bothers you or makes you jealous or anything, you're welcome to come too," Gwen offered.

"Don't be ridiculous," she dismissed the idea. "I wouldn't want to intrude."

"Are you sure?"

"Of course I'm sure. You and Dar are just friends. You'd never do anything to give me reason to be jealous, now would you?"

"I'm sorry, Beth," she declined guiltily. "But I've got too much work to do."

The silence was oppressive on the other end of the phone.

"We'll get together tomorrow night," she promised.

"I'm going to see my mother tomorrow. I won't be here."

Jane winced. She'd completely forgotten.

"So I guess maybe I'll see you Sunday then?" Beth's sad little voice wavered.

"Why don't you meet me at my place around eight?" Jane resigned her desk to its cluttered state.

"Do you know what you're going to do?"

Gwen shook her head. "What can I do? His father's latest unwed child bride doesn't want any part of him, and his mother headed for the hills long ago. I'd feel like the meanest bitch on earth to have to send him back to his grandparents again."

Darla nodded.

"I care about him and everything," she rationalized aloud. "But I've got my own life to live too."

Darla reached across the table to give her hand a little squeeze. "I know you do."

Gwen forced out a smile. "So what's going on with you?"

Darla grinned. Lately her brain was locked on two topics, Keely and sex, although she wasn't entirely certain the two subjects weren't one and the same.

"I've never seen you look happier, or Keely either," she observed. "I take it all's well in paradise?"

Darla laughed at her affectionate tease. "Pretty damned perfect," she agreed.

Gwen fell silent again.

"Thinking about Theron again?" she presumed.

"No. Actually I was thinking about Keely."

"What about her?"

Gwen debated.

"Come on," she pushed. "Out with it."

Gwen wasn't sure she should. "Has she always been crazy jealous?" she did anyway.

She regretted the words the instant they were out of her mouth. From the look on Dar's face, she'd just made a very big mistake.

"I'm sorry I'm late," she apologized.

"And I'm sorry I dragged you away from your work again," Beth's conscience got the better of her.

Jane flashed her a great big grin. "I'm not."

Beth felt better instantly.

Keely smiled as she got up off the sofa to answer the knock. It was eleven-thirty. There was only one person it could possibly be.

"How dare you tell Gwen to keep her hands off me?"

Keely's welcoming smile faded immediately. She stepped aside to let her obviously less-than-amused guest in.

"How dare you?" she repeated emphatically.

"I didn't tell her that," she scrambled.

"Maybe not in so many words, but you sure as hell got your point across," Darla barked. "I promised you I wouldn't screw around and, whether you like it or not, you're just going to have to trust me. I won't have you running around behind my back policing me or checking up on me or whatever the hell it is you think you're doing!"

Keely cringed. She was really angry. And maybe she had every right to be.

"You owe both Gwen and me an apology."

Keely retreated to the sofa.

"Well?" she demanded.

"You're right," she agreed. "I was out of line. I'm sorry."

Darla didn't know what to say. She hadn't expected her to concede the point so easily.

"I'll apologize to Gwen on Monday."

Darla scrutinized her closely. There wasn't a hint of insincerity on Keely's face. She really did see the stupidity of her jealousy.

"Why don't you come over here and sit down beside me?"

Darla wandered over to the window instead in a vain attempt at thermal regulation. "Is it really hot in here or am I just having another hot flash again?"

"It's warm," she confirmed.

Darla concentrated on ignoring the sensation. "Why don't you pack a few things and we'll go back to my place? It's air-conditioned there. In fact, why don't you pack this whole place and move in?"

Keely smiled but didn't say anything.

"I've already given you the ring," she tossed out. "Surely you're not expecting me to get down on one knee?"

Keely chuckled and then outright laughed as Darla lost control and broke into an out-and-out scratch.

"It's not funny," she growled. "I've got a hideous heat rash."

"Take the damned thing off then."

"I'd have to leave it off all weekend," she muttered. "It's going to take a couple of days to clear this disaster up."

Keely shrugged. "So? Why not?"

"Because my back will get really sore," she couldn't believe she had to explain yet again.

"Not if I keep you horizontal," she winked.

Darla smiled at her wicked little grin and then scowled again. "Tomorrow's highlight is dinner at your brother's," she wasn't looking forward to it in the least. "I can't exactly show up one-titted there."

"You said you'd go," Keely reminded her.

"I know," she grumbled. "I don't have to be happy about it though."

Keely smiled at her again. "Tell you what," she offered. "I'll run you a cool bath and I'll even get you a cold beer as consolation."

"Beer?" her ears perked up.

Keely nodded.

"Here?"

Keely nodded again.

"Why is there beer here?"

"Because I bought it for you," Keely laughed.

"You shouldn't have done that. I don't want you having beer in the house."

Keely laughed again.

"What's so funny?"

"You," she chuckled.

"What about me?" she failed to find anything about her concerns the least bit amusing.

"Now who's not trusting who?"

Jane jumped the puddle and continued up the path as it wound its way by the creek. She loved running in the morning when the dew was still on the grass and everyone else was still asleep. There wasn't another soul in sight but then she knew there wouldn't be. Nobody else in their right mind was up at six-thirty on a Saturday.

She sprinted the last hundred yards up the hill and then slowed to a fast walk, checking her pulse against her watch. She turned in the direction of home, smiling all the while. She wasn't just happy, she was ecstatic. Beth had finally deemed it meet-the-family time.

Darla stretched her arms over her head and yawned contentedly. Keely's apartment had cooled off at least a good ten degrees overnight.

"Your rash looks better this morning," she noted.

Darla watched Keely's finger slowly trace the length of her scar. "You miss it a lot, don't you?"

"Of course I miss it," Keely softly replied. "But

nowhere near as much as I'd miss the rest of you."

Darla kissed her on the top of the head.

"When you had your check-up did you have a mammogram?"

Keely's question took her off guard. She just shook her head.

"A bone scan?"

She shook her head again.

"Why not?" Keely persisted. "Don't they usually?"

Darla laughed. "When did you get to be such an expert?"

"I'm not an expert," she scowled. "I've just read a little."

Darla had a pretty good idea a little really meant a lot. She smiled.

"Well?"

"They didn't do a mammogram or a bone scan because I had them done when I was in the hospital," she patiently explained. "And besides, they didn't bother because I'm obviously so disgustingly healthy."

Keely looked at her dubiously.

"I never would have gotten re-involved with you if that wasn't true," Darla backed her statement in all seriousness. "You know that, don't you?"

She'd finally confirmed what Keely had suspected all along.

"Now, were you planning on actually making love with me or were you just taking inventory?"

Maureen Campbell finished stacking the dishes and poured a sinkful of soapy water. Jane smiled at Beth and disappeared into the den to watch the news like she was supposed to.

"Jane seems nice," she idly chatted.

Beth nodded. She thought so too.

Maureen put the glasses in the water. "Is she ... ? Are the two of you ... ?"

"Yes Mom," Beth rescued her as she floundered.

She nodded and moved the spout to fill the second sink with the rinse water. "What about the woman you're living with? What does she think of all of this?"

Beth smiled. "Dar and I aren't lovers Mom, we're friends."

Her clarification didn't elicit any response.

"Did you think we were?" she asked.

"I didn't think so," she replied. "But I was never really sure."

"I guess I should have told you," Beth decided.

"Maybe," Maureen agreed. "And maybe I should have asked you too."

Her mother's ready acceptance of partial responsibility for their lack of communication took Beth pleasantly by surprise.

"Is she a lesbian too? Dar, I mean."

Beth nodded. "And Jane too," she smirked.

Maureen looked at her daughter and giggled. "You have your father's sick sense of humour," she accused.

Beth grinned from ear to ear at the huge compliment.

"So what is it Jane does again?"

"She's a lawyer," she relayed.

"And how old is she?"

"Thirty-four. She'll be thirty-five in October."

Maureen nodded. "Are the two of you going to live together?"

Beth smiled at the predictability.

"Let me help you," Keely seized the opportunity and leaped to her feet. She finished clearing the table and followed her sister-in-law into the kitchen for a little private conversation.

"Do you think they'll kill each other?" Cindy giggled.

Keely smiled. "It's entirely possible."

"Brock promised to be on his best behaviour," she relayed. "I really hope he doesn't start anything."

"One thing's for sure," Keely snickered. "If he starts it, Dar will finish it."

Cindy opened the dishwasher.

"So?" Keely broached. "What do you think?"

"I think she's a very lucky woman to have you."

Keely bit the inside of her lip. She didn't like the sound of things. She was being far too diplomatic. "Is she what you expected?" she tried another tactic.

Cindy filled the top rack with glasses. "In some ways," she answered evasively.

"So you agree with Brock then," she concluded. "You don't like her either."

Cindy smiled at her disheartened look. "That's not true. I like her a lot. I think she has a great sense of humour and she's downright charming too."

Keely beamed.

"Although I must agree with Brock on one thing. She doesn't look anywhere near fifty."

"She's fifty-one," Keely corrected.

"And I guess he's right about one other thing too," she mused.

Keely looked at her apprehensively.

"She really is an advertisement for sex walking around on two feet."

Jane backed out of the driveway. "Did I do okay?"

Beth smiled at her insecurity and waved good-bye to her

mother. "You did wonderfully. And how did my mother do?"

Jane smiled. "I like her a lot. We should introduce her to Pete."

"Your father and my mother?" she stared at her in disbelief.

"Sure," Jane grinned. "Why not? Pete's really lonely and your mom must be too. After all, your dad's been dead for what now? Almost two years?"

Beth just looked at her. Either Jane was finally losing it or her well-hidden sense of humour was extremely twisted.

"How old is Maureen anyway?"

"Sixty-five. No, sixty-six."

Jane considered it. "That's not bad," she concluded. "Pete's sixty-three."

"You're nuts!" Beth dismissed her.

"Oh, come on. All I suggested was introducing them. What's the matter with that?"

"It's sick," Beth proclaimed. "Bordering on the twisted."

Jane broke into gales of laughter.

"What's so funny?"

"You calling the idea of your mother and my father getting together twisted," she choked out. "That's what."

"Well, it is!" Beth protested adamantly.

"This coming from a woman who is current sleeping with her ex-lover's other ex-lover? From a woman who used to live with her lover *and* her lover's other lover too? Come on, Beth," Jane implored her. "You've got to admit your reaction is more than a little funny. It's hilarious."

"It's freezing in here," Keely complained. "How low have you got the damned thermostat set anyway?"

Darla cuddled up beside her.

"I suppose you're hot," Keely muttered.

Darla bit her neck. "Aren't I?" she checked.

Keely smiled. "Brock certainly seems to think so."

"What?"

"Cindy told me tonight that Brock said you're an ad for sex on two feet."

Darla laughed appreciatively. "I like Cindy," she decided.

"She likes you too."

"Brock still hates me though," she pouted.

"No, he doesn't," Keely countered. "He just doesn't understand a lot of the stuff that's gone on between us."

"Sometimes I don't either," she reflected in all honesty.

Keely smiled and closed her eyes. She was really tired.

"Why did you come and see me before Christmas?" she asked out of the blue. "And don't say it was just because Beth asked you to."

Keely didn't know how to compress so many hours of soul-searching into one neat and tidy little explanation. "I guess maybe I just wanted to finally say the words 'I love you'," she decided after a good long think.

Darla smiled and turned out the light.

"Did madame not find my answer satisfactory?"

Darla's kiss confirmed it was very satisfactory indeed.

Beth bit at the rough edge of her nail. "Do you have a nail file or clippers or anything?" she called to her in the bathroom.

"Top drawer of the night stand on my side of the bed."

Beth rolled across the bed to retrieve them. She opened the drawer and smiled at the orderliness of the contents. Neat-freak Jane's touch was everywhere. She trimmed her broken nail and set them back in the drawer beside the pile of books.

"Did you find them?"

"Yes, thank you," she answered, giving the reading material a closer look. There was a book on pregnancy and one on natural childbirth, as well as several handwritten pages on artificial insemination. Beth slammed the drawer firmly shut.

"Not you too," she groaned.

Darla looked up from her desk.

"Working on a Sunday," she pissed and moaned. "How could you?"

"The plaintive call of the workaholic's lonely spousal equivalent," Darla identified her whine. "Deserted for the gratifications of the office once again."

Beth invited herself in and flopped into a chair.

"And other than the agony of today's rejection, how was your weekend?"

"I went to visit my mom yesterday," she recounted. "And I took Jane."

"My, my, my," she smirked. "Getting serious, aren't we? Seeking matriarchal approval and everything."

Beth rolled her eyes.

"Hark?" she brought her hand to her ear. "Is that wedding bells I hear a-ringing?"

"Don't be looking at me," she laughed off even the possibility. "You're the one who's been handing out rings."

Darla grinned. "So now that we've done our approach by introducing the prospective mate to Mom, we're firmly back in avoid mode again?"

Beth screwed up her face. "I think Jane's really serious about the baby thing."

"Time to pack our toys and go somewhere else to play?"

"Something like that," she readily agreed.

"Ah. The work of the true commitment-phobe is never done. I am, of course, totally reformed, although Keely is displaying tendencies these days. She has once again abandoned me for the pleasures of her own company."

"Afraid we're going to be left standing at the altar?" she surmised.

Darla couldn't disagree.

"So what do you suppose two pathetic excuses for human beings could find to do together today?"

"I don't know," she shrugged. "Want to see my scar?"

"I've seen it," Beth snickered. "You'll have to do better than that."

"I could show it to you in the bedroom," she proposed.

Beth laughed and shook her head. "Why don't we make a pitcher of margaritas instead?"

"We didn't get either job then?"

He shook his head and went back to looking dejected again.

"We thought we were sunk last year and we survived," Keely reminded him. "Something will turn up. It always does."

Brock laughed. "Since when are you so upbeat and positive?"

She shrugged. "Why not? I'll check with Dar and see if she knows anything."

He wasn't about to protest. At this point he'd take the work from anywhere.

"Oh. That reminds me," she just had to. "Dar said to tell you that she thinks you're sexy too."

"So what about dinner?" Jane asked for the second time.

Beth shrugged. "Dar's in the tub. Let me ask her what she and Keely are doing."

Jane sighed and poured herself another glass of wine. These en masse decisions always took forever.

"Are you going out or staying in for dinner?" Beth called through the bathroom door.

"I don't know," she replied. "I haven't talked to Keely since yesterday morning."

Beth returned to the kitchen. "She's not sure what she's doing."

Jane nodded and took another sip of wine. "Doesn't it drive you crazy?" she couldn't believe it wouldn't.

"What?"

"All the coming and going and never knowing what's going on."

Beth smiled. "I've always kind of liked it."

Jane shook her head. She didn't. Not one little bit. As far as she was concerned, the entire household qualified as an insane asylum.

"Let's stay in," Beth decided.

"Hello, you two," Keely wandered into the kitchen after letting herself in. "What's going on?"

Jane rolled her eyes. Another complication.

"We were just trying to decide what to do about dinner," Beth filled her in.

Keely nodded. "Where's Dar?"

"In the tub," Jane wearily provided.

Keely promptly disappeared into the bathroom. "Hello, Old Girl," she greeted her. "How was your day?"

Darla smiled. "Simply divine. The bike shop called. The Harley's ready."

Keely shook her head and plunked down on the edge

of the tub. Whether she liked it or not, the overgrown adolescent was going to ride again.

"And how was your day at work?"

Keely shrugged. "I survived. I've still got all ten toes and nine and a bit fingers, but I'm getting too old for this shit."

Darla smiled at her case of the pits. "Don't I get a kiss?"

Keely leaned over obligingly. Darla promptly pulled her into the tub. Keely's holler could be heard for miles. Jane looked at Beth for an explanation.

"My best guess is that Keely just got rudely invited into the bath water."

There was a resurgence in the laughter from the bathroom. Jane got up from the table.

"Where are you going?" Beth called after her.

"Somewhere more sane," she replied, closing the door behind her.

Gwen put down the screw gun and smiled at Theron. "I'll be back in a minute, big guy. Keep doing what you're doing."

Theron scowled and carried on mudding the drywall. First Keely had buggered off and now Gwen too. He was a second-class citizen. Slave labour. He was almost looking forward to going back to school.

"How's he doing?" Keely status-checked.

"Okay," she shrugged. "He's crabby because I took a break. But he'll get over it," she laughed. "You were right. A little hard work has done him a world of good."

"No more repeats of the drinking?"

Gwen shook her head. "But I still haven't decided what to do about him. Dar thinks I should talk to a lawyer."

Keely nodded. She thought so too.

"Don't you two ever do any work?"

"Never," Keely smiled. "We while our days away standing around chatting."

"I suppose you've got poor Theron chained to his post," Darla surmised. "I came by to borrow him for the rest of the day. What do you say?"

Keely looked at Gwen, leaving the decision up to her.

"Sure," she shrugged. "What are the two of you going to do?"

"Go for a bike ride," Darla announced. "I promised him we would."

"Hey, Theron!" Keely called. "Dar's here to see you."

He stuck his head out the door. "Hi, Dar. How are you?"

"Better now that I've seen you."

He giggled and tried very hard not to turn red.

Darla tossed him the helmet. "Come on, big guy. Let's go for a ride."

"Oh, wow!" he gushed ecstatically. "I didn't think you remembered."

"Of course I did," she grinned. "A promise is a promise. We'll meet you back at the house later," she called back to them.

Keely watched their antics as Theron and Dar got ready to take off on the bike. He dusted himself off before he donned Keely's old leather jacket and pulled the helmet on. The Harley roared to life and Theron eagerly climbed on behind her. Keely smiled. They made quite a pair, a fourteen-year-old kid in too big a hurry to grow up and a fifty-one-year-old perpetual adolescent.

"Jane Tolliver," she mechanically answered her phone.

"Hi, Jane Tolliver. It's me."

Jane smiled at her obvious good mood.

"Did I call at a bad time? I hope I'm not interrupting you?"

"It's okay, Beth," Jane assured her. "I'm busy but, after all, you are my favourite distraction."

Beth giggled.

"So what's up? Did you just call to chat?"

"No. I was calling to see if you had any plans for tonight."

Jane stared at the pile of papers on the desk and her plans for the evening promptly stared back.

"I hope you don't," Beth ventured. "Because I thought I might make you a nice romantic dinner tonight. Just the two of us. What do you say? Is it a date?"

Jane smiled. What could she say? The lawyer needed to work, but the romantic needed to go to dinner. "Okay," she caved in. "But I won't be able to come over until around eight."

"What are you grinning about?"

"Nothing," she shook her off.

"Come on," Darla poked her again.

Keely turned around and gestured towards the deck. "Gwen," she smirked.

"What about her?"

"Take a look," Keely directed.

Gwen was sitting beside Beth, clearly enthralled by more than just their conversation. Darla smiled too.

"Do you know what Gwen asked me when we went to pick up the pizza?" she chuckled.

Darla shook her head.

"She asked me what my secret is for meeting such interesting women."

Jane scowled when she pulled in the driveway. Just the two of us appeared to have been a gross underestimation. Not only were Dar's car and Keely's truck there, but there was another one too. She climbed the stairs and knocked on the door. Beth opened it eventually and greeted her without so much as a kiss.

"Having an impromptu party, are we?" she gathered from the cast of characters lounging about on the back deck.

Beth shook her head. "It's just Dar and Keely and Gwen and Theron. They all kind of just showed up," she tried to explain.

Jane put her briefcase down. So now the evening had turned into an intimate little get-together for six.

"Could you do me a favour?" Beth broached. "Would you talk to Gwen for a few minutes about how she might go about getting financial support for Theron?"

Jane rolled her eyes. What next?

"I know you've had a long day," she attempted to placate. "I'll get you a beer?" she bribed her. "And a slice of pizza?"

And now a nice dinner had been down-scaled to pizza. She'd put in a twelve-hour day and she had a pretty good idea the evening was going to seem even longer.

"Jane?"

She rolled over and opened her eyes.

"Jane?" she paged again. "Are you awake?"

"I am now," she grumbled.

Keely quietly climbed the last three stairs. "I'm sorry," she offered. "But your car's behind my truck. If you give me your keys, I'll move it," she tried to soften the blow.

"They're in my briefcase by the door," she growled.

Jane lay back down again upon Keely's hasty retreat. She heard the door close and Keely thump down the stairs. Then there was the sound of her car starting, followed by Keely's truck, then Keely coming back up the stairs and closing the door again. She shut her eyes and started to drift back into dreamland. The door banged again. Someone, undoubtedly Dar, descended the stairs and then started her car. She rolled onto her side to face the sleeping woman beside her. It was two-thirty in the morning and it just wasn't fair. She kissed her. Beth moaned in her sleep. She kissed her again. Beth groaned and opened her eyes. She kissed her yet again. Beth smiled and put her arms around her.

"I'm going to work now."

Darla opened her eyes and smiled. Keely leaned over and kissed her.

"I love you," she said, all soft and sleepy.

Keely smiled. "I love you too."

Darla sat up and kissed her again. "Why don't you come home for lunch?" she suggested playfully.

Keely laughed. "It sounds like a plan to me."

Jane looked up at the soft rap on the door.

"I'm sorry," she apologized. "I know you said you didn't want to be disturbed but there's a woman here insisting on seeing you. Her name is Dr. Campbell. She says she's your gynecologist," the receptionist smirked. "Shall I send her in?"

Jane turned a thousand shades of red and nodded her head. Beth strolled into her office brandishing a self-satisfied grin.

"Now it's about that internal, Ms. Tolliver," she opened.

Jane quickly scrambled to close her door.

"Oh, relax," Beth encouraged her. "It will give them all something to talk about."

"My interest in certain types of cases already does enough of that!"

Beth was taken aback. She didn't expect her to be so angry. In fact, she'd thought Jane would find the whole thing funny.

"What are you doing here anyway?"

"I came to take you to lunch."

"Well, I'm too busy," Jane dismissed the idea.

"Can't you make an hour for me?"

"That's why I'm so busy in the first place," she snapped. "I've been making too many hours for you."

Beth paused to regroup. "You're certainly in foul humour today."

"Well, excuse me! I'm tired."

"As if that's my fault," Beth pointed out. "As I recall you were the one who woke me up in the middle of the night last night."

"Only because your crazy friends woke me up first," she countered.

"Oh, I see," Beth seethed. "You woke me up because you were awake anyway and didn't have anything better to do? Is that it?"

Jane sighed in frustration. "Beth, I'm really busy. I don't have time to argue with you."

"Fine! And a fuck you to you too!" she blew. "Far be it from me to keep Her Ladyship from her work!"

The entire office watched Beth storm out the door.

"But I don't get it," Keely responded, totally baffled by Dar's second-hand account. "Beth and Jane really love each other. Why would they split up over a silly little argument like that?"

Darla smiled. "Because it's as good an excuse as any."

Now Keely was even further confused.

"Beth doesn't want to get caught," Darla illuminated.

"Caught?"

"Trapped into playing house with down-to-earth Jane and their future baby."

"Huh?"

Darla shrugged. "She wants a little more craziness."

"If it's craziness she wants, she should have married you."

Darla laughed. "That's probably true. But unfortunately the only one either of us has ever been interested in trapping is you."

"Funny," Keely remarked. "I remember the old days more as me trying to snag you."

"Ah," Darla smiled. "But that was before I realized the silliness of the game. Neither of us ever managed to win, and it hurt like hell for us both to lose."

Keely wondered if, for once, she was actually being serious, but as usual it was hard to tell.

"When are you going to let me reel you into living with me?" she bantered ambiguously. "Or haven't I caught you yet?"

Keely laughed. "Tell you what," she offered playfully. "First I'll catch you," she advised with a kiss. "And then I'll let you catch me."

August

"I'm healed," she announced.

Darla sure as hell hoped so. Beth's pissed-off-and-toxic routine had given way to a silent sulk when Jane still hadn't called after a whole two weeks. Anything had to be better than that.

"Things weren't going to work out with Jane anyway," she explained. "Maybe I'll take a page out of your book and buy the sports car I've always wanted to cheer myself up," she beamed. "And who knows? Maybe I'll find some cute young thing to put in it too?"

Darla smiled. "Sounds like the perfect mid-life crisis plan to me. Have you got any particular woman in mind?"

Beth shook her head. "Actually, with my track record I was wondering if I shouldn't give some serious consideration to the concept of men. What do you think?"

"Definitely not," Darla laughed at the absurdity. "But the sports car? Now that has possibilities."

"So where is she?"

Darla shrugged. "All the note says is that she went out and that she probably won't be late."

"I guess that means she's not with Jane," Keely concluded unhappily. "Do you think they'll make up?"

Darla shook her head doubtfully. "Not from what Beth said this morning," she relayed.

Keely yawned again. "I don't know about you, but I'm ready for bed."

"Okay," she readily agreed. "And maybe if you're lucky I'll actually let you get some sleep."

Beth locked the door behind her and tiptoed into the dark kitchen in search of a much-needed drink. She grabbed a glass and extracted the Scotch from the cupboard above the sink.

"Where the hell were you?"

Beth dropped her glass at the startle. She hadn't seen her sitting there.

"I'm sorry I scared you," she hushed her voice. "But it's four thirty in the morning and you had me worried."

Beth picked up her glass and opened the freezer. "Thanks for waiting up, Mom," she jabbed good-naturedly.

Darla got up to procure a glass of her own and met her at the kitchen table. Beth poured both drinks. Dar always did like her Scotch neat.

"So where were you?"

"Like I said in the note, I went out."

"Did you and the good counsellor get together to talk?" she wondered from the late hour.

"Hardly," Beth dismissed the possibility. "I went out with Gwen," she grinned conspiratorially.

Darla smiled. Both cute and young were rather apt descriptions. "Had a nice time, did we?"

"Yeah," her smile grew even wider. "We did."

It only took Darla a moment to add two plus two. "You slept with her."

Beth fairly beamed.

"Well, I'll be," she chuckled. "And how was it?"

"You ought to know."

"Me? How would I know? Ms. McFadden and I never made it remotely near a bed. Should we have?" she wondered wickedly.

Beth rose from the table. "Let's put it this way," she shared on her way to the stairs. "I think Ms. McFadden and I will be seeing each other again."

Beth could still hear her stifled laughter from upstairs. "Dar?" she called down to her in a strained whisper.

"Yes, Cassie-nova?"

"Don't tell Keely."

"I won't. Good night."

Keely stumbled into the kitchen in the middle of a yawn. "I woke up and you were gone."

"Poor baby," Darla consoled her. "Waking up in a strange place all alone."

Keely smiled. Neither Dar's bed or her house exactly qualified as foreign. She knew exactly where she was before she opened her eyes. She went over to the counter to get a coffee.

"Yes, please," Darla paged for a refill. "So what do you want to do today?"

Keely poured and shrugged. She hadn't thought that far ahead.

"Gail called me this week," she chatted. "The price on that lot we saw on your birthday has dropped."

Keely shook her head. A one-night stand turned real estate agent. What next? Sometimes it was just too small a community.

"So what do you think?" she inquired. "You've seen the drawings for the house. I think it's a fairly ideal lot, don't you?"

"It's way the hell out in the middle of nowhere," Keely pointed out.

"I've always wanted to live in the country," she started to pout.

"It's up to you," Keely abdicated. "It's your house."

Darla fell silent and the palms of her hands started to sweat. There was no easy way. "I want it to be your house too," she eventually made herself say.

"I know you do," she acknowledged. "But right now next year feels like it's a million miles away. I'm still working on handling things day by day."

Darla smiled at the irony. The shoe truly was on the other foot this time. She was the one pushing, and Keely was the one with all the excuses for running away.

"Are you upset?" Keely checked.

"Not at all," she lied. "Now what did you want to do today?"

"Well, I hate to eat and run," Beth excused herself, "but I've got to go."

Keely looked after her up the stairs. "She's avoiding me."

"Oh, Keely," Darla intercepted. "Stop being so paranoid."

"Well, what am I supposed to think? She was upstairs all day."

"Maybe she was just asleep?"

"Yeah, right," Keely rejected the suggestion. "And she only woke up in time to come downstairs and have dinner. Come on, Dar! You know better than that."

Darla maintained what she hoped was a blank expression.

"And now all of a sudden she's got somewhere else to go. She is avoiding me," Keely declared with even more certainty.

Darla smiled. "Did you ever think maybe she's got a date?"

Keely brightened. "Did she make up with Jane?"

Darla shook her head. "Maybe she's seeing somebody else?" she hinted.

"Oh, yeah? Like who?"

Darla raised an eyebrow, making her position perfectly clear. She knew who it was but she wasn't saying.

"Come on, Dar," she pushed her.

She firmly shook her head.

"But you know who it is, don't you?"

She smiled and nodded.

"At least give me a clue," Keely whined.

Darla took a moment to consider. "It's someone I went out with a time or two."

Keely rolled her eyes. "Great clue, Dar. You've been out with three-quarters of the damned community."

Beth bounded down the stairs two at a time, taking a detour into the kitchen to kiss both of them on the top of the head as they sat at the table.

"Have a good time," Darla wished her and winked.

Beth broke into a big grin.

"Should I wait up?" Keely lightly inquired. "Is this mystery date of yours a trustworthy sort?"

"I don't know, Keely," Beth laughed. "You tell me."

The knock at the door intensified Keely's baffled look.

"I'd better go," Beth decided and was off in a flash. Gwen would just have to understand why she wasn't getting invited in.

Keely was really disappointed. She thought she was going to get to meet her. "So I gather from Beth's last remark it's somebody I know?" she tried to put the pieces together.

"And that," Darla pointed out. "Narrows it down to about half the community."

Gwen's kiss had her full and undivided attention, so much so that she didn't even see her standing at the bar until it was far too late. They made eye contact and held it for a moment before Jane looked away.

"What's the matter?" Gwen read the change in climate.

Beth watched her down the rest of her beer and then move in the direction of the back door.

"Beth?"

"Just a second," Beth dismissed her and took off in hot pursuit. By the time she caught up with her she was already halfway down the stairs.

"Jane?" she called after her.

She didn't stop, she didn't turn. She just kept on descending the flight.

"Jane, please!"

She opened the door and stepped out into the alley. She was halfway to the street before Beth grabbed her arm from behind.

"I want to talk to you," she insisted.

Jane turned around to face her, totally expressionless. "Okay. So talk."

Jane's eyes were as cold as steel. All of a sudden Beth didn't have any words to say.

"You'd better get back," Jane eventually broke the silence. "I'm sure Gwen's wondering where you've gone."

Beth stood and watched her walk away down the alley.

Keely gently lifted Dar's arm and slipped out from under it. Times had changed. Now Dar was the one who instantly fell asleep. She pulled on her jeans and T-shirt and headed to the back deck, anxious for a post-orgasmic smoke.

She leaned against the railing to enjoy her cigarette under a full moon. It was a beautiful evening. She looked back inside at the sound of someone in the kitchen.

Beth poured herself a liberal Scotch on the rocks. She needed a drink for the second night in a row. She leaned back against the counter to put a major dent in it and then turned to the patio door, feeling rather than hearing someone's presence behind her. Keely smiled at her in the moonlight. Beth hesitated and then joined her.

"So how was your date?"

"The shits," Beth assessed. "I just told her I don't think we should see each other again."

"You didn't get along?"

"No. I wish it was that."

Keely didn't know what to do or say next. She was clearly deeply upset. "Can I help?" she offered.

Beth did her best not to cry.

"Talk to me," she encouraged.

Beth looked up at her. "I went to the bar tonight."

"And you ran into Jane?" she guessed.

Beth nodded. "Of course I didn't know she was there until it was too late."

Keely waited.

"I was very busily kissing ... someone else," she saw no reason to mention Gwen's name, "when she walked in."

Keely winced. "And?"

"And then she took off and I went after her."

"And?" Keely prompted again.

Beth shivered as Jane's cold stare haunted her once more.

"Did the two of you talk?"

"I tried to but I didn't have anything to say, and now I just can't get the look she had on her face out of my mind."

"You're upset because you hurt her," she assumed.

Beth sadly shook her head. "I'm upset because I realized how much I love her and how badly I fucked up."

Keely's heart ached for her at the appearance of her tears.

"I don't know why I have to be such a fuck-up," she wept. "I made exactly the same stupid mistake with her that I made with you."

Keely put her arm around her in silent reassurance.

"Oh, Keely," she sobbed. "Why can't I ever seem to learn? Why did I have to do it again? It hurts just as much as when I lost you."

Keely brought her hand to the back of Beth's head and gathered her closer to hold her tight.

She froze when she saw them standing there, holding each other in the moonlight. Her heart pounded. She clenched her fists at her sides in an attempt to stave off the scream mounting inside of her. It just couldn't be happening again.

Keely leaned down to kiss Beth on the forehead, transforming her anger and frustration into tears of desolation. Darla couldn't bear to just stand there and watch the inevitable happen. She quietly vanished back into the bedroom, leaving them oblivious to the fact that she was ever there.

Beth placed the receiver back in the cradle at the sound of the dial tone. Jane had made herself abundantly clear. She wasn't to call again.

She sighed and closed her eyes. At least she'd tried. There was nothing else she could do except let herself cry.

"Hey, Old Girl. Stop hogging all the hot water."

Darla rinsed her hair and turned sideways to slip by

her. The opportunity was too good to miss, as far as Keely was concerned. She cornered her and kissed her. Darla put her arms around her and tried very hard not to cry.

"What's the matter?" Keely read the signs.

"Nothing," she shook her head. "I just really love you."

Keely smiled and held her all the tighter.

"Did Keely go home?"

"Sorry to disappoint you, but yes."

Beth sighed and sat down at the kitchen table. "Are you angry because I talked to Keely last night instead of you?"

Darla scowled.

"Dar?"

She shook her head. "I'm just in a shitty mood."

"Then you're upset because Keely went home," Beth second-guessed.

"Right," she snipped. "That's exactly it. Thank you for your divine insight once again."

Beth promptly shut up and left the room.

Keely spent her morning trying to stay out of Gwen's way and Theron did too, although less successfully. Keely felt sorry for the poor kid. No matter how hard he tried, he just couldn't seem to do anything right.

"You're being too hard on him," she finally just had to intervene.

"Fine. Then you handle him!" Gwen snapped.

Keely watched her stomp outside and then looked back at Theron.

"Don't look at me," he shrugged. "She's been as bitchy as hell since the moment she got up yesterday."

Keely eyed him dubiously.

"Honest," he squirmed. "It wasn't me this time. I didn't do anything."

"Okay, then," she gave in. "Why don't you take a break while I go and talk to her?"

"You better take this," he warned.

Keely laughed and took the hard hat from his outstretched hand before going after her. "What's with the mood?" she got right to it.

Gwen scowled at the ground.

"Theron says he didn't do anything."

"He didn't," she conceded.

"Then what are you so mad about?"

Gwen looked up at her incredulously. "You really don't know, do you?" she realized.

"Know what?"

"Nothing," Gwen said. "But do me a favour and don't ever introduce me to any of your ex-lovers again."

September

"Maybe I just want to have a bath alone? Okay?" she roared.

"Okay, okay," Keely gave up in defeat and retreated into the kitchen. "Jesus, she's in one foul mood," she muttered to Beth.

"I wouldn't take it personally," she advised. "She's been like this for days."

"Gwen too," Keely complained.

Beth squirmed uncomfortably at the mere mention of her name.

"And I suppose you've got an ugly on too?"

Beth smiled and shook her head. "I'm still wallowing in my feeling-sorry-for-myself phase. I'm too depressed to be cranky."

Keely laughed. At least one of the three still had her sense of humour.

"Keely, don't," she pulled away. "I'm tired and I've got a headache."

"Satisfaction or your money cheerfully refunded," she lightly guaranteed.

"I said no and I mean no," she adamantly restated.

Keely rolled over and turned out the light. No was getting to be Dar's favourite word.

"If you're so goddamned horny then why don't you just

go upstairs? There's a perfectly healthy woman with two rather lovely breasts just waiting for you there."

Keely sat bolt upright. "Is that what this is all about? Are you jealous of Beth?"

"You're damned right I am! And don't try and deny it, Keely. We both know I have good reason to be!"

"What the hell is that supposed to mean?"

"Just that," Darla snapped. "You don't have to pretend any more. I saw you."

"I don't know what you think you saw, but you're wrong!"

"What about that night on the deck?"

"All you saw was Beth being really upset about Jane," she couldn't believe she had to explain. "I did not and I will not sleep with Beth or anybody else who has two breasts. You happen to be the only one I'm interested in, although lord knows why."

Darla started to cry. Keely lay back down and put her arm around her.

"Then why won't you live with me?" she whimpered.

Keely sighed. This again.

"If you loved me you'd want to live with me," she whined.

"I do love you, Dar. That has absolutely nothing to do with why I won't live with you."

"Then why won't you?" she sniffled.

"Because I'm not ready to do that yet."

"You don't trust me," she pouted. "You think I'll screw it up again."

Keely shook her head. "If anybody's likely to screw up this time, it's me," she answered honestly. "I haven't had a drink since last December, but I came damned close in the spring."

"You fell off the wagon in December because of me," she stated with certainty.

"And in the spring I came close because of you going

out with Gwen. Since we've gotten back together it's been easy. But I need to know that I can stay sober all on my own, without you. I've got to learn that I can trust me."

"And when you find out you can?" she broached cautiously.

"You'll be the first to know," Keely promised. "You won't be able to get rid of me."

"I'm sorry I've been such a bitch lately."

Beth smiled at her over the top of her book. "Did Keely go home?"

Darla nodded and sat on the end of Beth's bed.

"She didn't go to work today?"

She shook her head. "We were up half the night. She was beat."

"Another marathon session?" Beth teased.

"No, actually. We were talking."

"About?"

"About my being jealous of you," Darla relayed. "I thought you and Keely were sleeping together again."

"You honestly thought Keely and I ... ?"

She nodded.

Beth laughed. "No wonder you've been so bitchy. Where would you get a crazy idea like that?"

"From a vivid imagination fuelled by massive insecurity," she furnished. "Forgive me?"

"Of course I do. But you have to know that I wouldn't do that to you. I know how important working things out with Keely is to you."

"So you're saying it never crossed your mind?"

"I'll admit I was pretty upset at first when the two of you got back together," she replied truthfully. "But I'm over that."

Darla nodded.

"Would it be easier for you if I moved out?"

"Absolutely not. I wouldn't know what to do without you. Although it's a good thing you didn't ask me that last week."

Beth smiled. "You and Keely really do belong together," she furthered. "I hope you manage to work things out permanently this time."

Darla got up off the bed. "Thank you. Me too."

Beth's attention drifted back to the text in front of her again.

"I love you," she said.

Beth grinned up at her. "I love you too."

"You and Jane belong together too," she duly informed her and set off down the steps.

Beth sighed and set her book aside. Sometimes she just hated it when Dar was right.

"Is Dar your girlfriend?"

Keely smiled at him and nodded.

"Have you been going out for very long?"

Keely's smile grew. "I fell in love with Dar when I wasn't much older than you."

His jaw dropped in disbelief. "And you don't live together yet?"

Keely laughed and shook her head. "We're working on it," she promised.

Theron took a bite of his sandwich. He liked Keely and he liked working Saturdays too. Gwen wasn't there to bug him.

"So what about you?" Keely turned the tables. "Have you got a girlfriend too?"

He smiled and turned ruby red.

"What's her name?"

"Melissa," he pined.

Keely struggled to hide her amusement with the entire conversation.

"How many times did you go out with Dar before you kissed her?" he mustered all his courage to ask.

Keely couldn't help herself. She just had to laugh.

"It was really nice of Keely to give Theron a job on Saturdays," she mentioned.

Darla nodded. "She's so busy right now it feels like I hardly see her. But that's okay," she decided. "Not that long ago she was afraid the business was going under."

Gwen scowled. "She didn't say anything to me."

"She didn't want to worry you."

Gwen took a sip of her coffee. "Did I tell you Jane's working on getting me official custody and support for Theron?"

She nodded.

"And that she's doing it for free?"

Darla shook her head. "I knew Jane was nice but that's a little ridiculous."

"No kidding," she agreed. "Especially after my part in what happened between her and Beth."

"Don't write them off yet," Darla advised. "Beth hasn't."

Gwen smiled. "Jane's so pissy about the entire topic, I don't think she has either. She told me if I even so much as mention Beth she'll charge me her full fee."

"How come you're so quiet this morning? Got a headache again?"

Darla chuckled. "Hardly," she dismissed her tease.

Keely kissed her forehead anyway. She wasn't taking any chances.

"That's not where it hurts," she set her up wickedly.

Keely looked at her worriedly.

"I think it's my mouth that needs to be kissed better," she winked.

Keely obliged only too willingly.

"Actually I think it's lower," she reconsidered.

Keely leaned over and kissed her throat. "Here?"

"Uh-uh," she shook her head.

Keely kissed her mastectomy scar.

"Not there either," Darla decided.

Keely nibbled her hip. "Here?" she suggested playfully.

"No, lover," she smiled. "But you're getting warmer."

Keely changed position again.

"That's it," she stroked her hair contentedly. "That's the spot exactly."

"I fucked up royally, didn't I?"

There was no need for a reply. The question was rhetorical anyway. Beth sat down on the grass to soak up the fall sunshine.

"I called Jane again," she shared. "I thought it was worth one more try." She took a deep breath. "It's over," she admitted dejectedly.

The silence was just too depressing. Beth got to her feet again.

"I love you, Wally," she told her dear friend.

"I love you too, sweetie," he answered in her head. "Everything will turn out, you'll see."

She smiled at the memory.

The End

December 1991

DARLA TURNED THE windshield wipers on against the snow. She changed the station on the radio and then switched it again. It was the third Christmas carol in a row. She pulled up to the red light and glanced in her rearview mirror.

"Merry Christmas," she wished herself. "Ho fucking ho."

"I am not drinking again!" she denied his accusation vehemently.

"Well, what the hell am I supposed to think? You couldn't be bothered coming to work yesterday and now you show up today two hours late, looking like a total bag of shit."

"I called you yesterday," Keely defended herself.

"Yes, you're quite right. And with such a great explanation too. 'I won't be in' doesn't tell me a lot, now does it? So what the hell's going on?"

Keely looked at the floor and swallowed.

"This has got something to do with Darla, doesn't it?" Brock knew it just had to. "That woman's been nothing but trouble for you."

She tried really hard not to cry.

"Oh, Keely," he sighed. "What happened between you two this time?"

February

DARLA SAT IN the hair stylist's chair brandishing a big frown, while Beth stood beside her looking on.

"I hate waiting," she pouted.

Beth smiled.

"What the hell's taking so long?"

"Darla, darling," Reynaldo flitted around the corner. "And dear Beth too," he pronounced with a flounce. "Do I get the pleasure of cutting both gorgeous heads today or just yours?"

"Just mine," Darla muttered crankily.

Reynaldo hummed to himself as he pawed through her wet hair. "What were they doing back there?" he flew into a snit. "They didn't colour it!"

"Take a downer," Darla advised. "I told them not to."

"Oh," he recovered. "Going au naturelle, are we?"

"Au naturelle," she confirmed. "And extremely short."

"Short?" his eyes lit up at being allowed to do what he'd always wanted to. "How short?"

"Very short," she instructed.

"Above the ears?" he fantasized.

Darla nodded.

Reynaldo picked up his scissors and took the first chop. Beth turned away as the foot-long strand hit the floor silently. She couldn't bear to watch.

"Do you know Meg O'Reilly?" Gwen dropped from out of the blue.

"Uh-huh," Keely replied. "I haven't seen her in years though."

"Do you know her very well?"

Keely shook her head. "Not really."

Gwen broke into a great big grin. She'd finally found a nice woman who wasn't one of Keely's ex-lovers.

"Sleeping more secure these days?"

Gwen looked at her blankly.

"You know what they say," she teased. "Sleep secure. Sleep with a cop."

Gwen blushed beet red at having been caught. Keely's attention shifted back to her cigarette. Silence enveloped them again.

"Are you okay?" she checked.

Keely attempted a smile. "I'm just having a bad day."

Gwen watched her put out her cigarette and walk away. That was the only kind of day her boss was having lately.

"I bought something today."

Darla remained buried behind her newspaper.

"Something to cheer us both up," Beth explained. "A little happy birthday to me."

Darla looked up at her expectantly.

"It's in the driveway," she grinned.

Darla was at the window immediately. "The red's certainly a statement," she granted.

Beth beamed proudly.

"And a convertible no less," she approved entirely. Darla smiled for the first time in weeks. "Let's put the top down and go for a ride."

Beth laughed. "That's exactly what I had in mind."

April

JANE GLANCED UP at the approaching couple walking arm in arm down the street. She turned to say something to her companion before stopping short and looking again.

"Jane," Keely greeted her. "Long time no see."

She managed to produce a smile despite the shock. "I'm forgetting my manners," she recovered quickly. "This is Lynn," she introduced. "And this is Dar and Keely."

Everyone smiled and nodded in each other's direction.

"You've been ill," Jane brought the obvious to the fore. "I'm sorry, I didn't know."

"Hard to believe, isn't it?" Darla smirked. "Lucky me. I've got breast cancer again."

"Had," Keely firmly corrected.

Darla ran her fingers through what was left of her grey hair. "Oh, look," she snickered, handing Keely a clump. "More for your collection, lover."

Keely smiled at the appalled look on Lynn's face and stuffed it in her pocket.

"I'm running a lottery," Darla explained. "I'm taking bets on by what date I'll be totally bald. I'm already most of the way there after only six weeks of chemotherapy. Any guesses, counsellor?"

Jane just had to laugh. She'd really missed Dar and her irreverent sense of humour.

"Keely guessed April Fools' Day," she went on. "So she's already out of the running. Shall I put you down for sometime in May?"

Jane shook her head. "I'd be willing to bet you're never going to lose it entirely."

Darla smiled at her. "You're very sweet."

"We were just on our way to the bar for a drink," Jane covered her embarrassment well. "Care to join us?"

"No, thanks," Keely declined. "Dar's really tired. I'm going to take her home and put her to bed."

"Promises, promises," Darla nudged her playfully.

"Well, good night then," Jane wished them. "You two take care."

"Yeah," Keely smiled. "You too."

Both couples carried on in opposite directions.

"So how do you know them?" Lynn probed.

"They're kind of friends of a friend," Jane relayed. She stopped dead in her tracks. "I'll be back in a second," she announced and turned to run back up the street. "Dar?" she called after her.

Darla leaned against the open passenger door of the Mercedes and waited. Jane walked the last few steps in an attempt to catch her breath.

"I just wanted to ask you about Beth. How is she?"

Darla smiled. "Oh, she's okay. She's busy right now with it being the end of the semester."

Jane nodded. "Tell her ... tell her I said hello."

"I will, Jane."

Jane nodded again. "Thanks, then," she terminated the conversation. "Good night."

Darla got in and closed the door behind her. Keely pulled away from the curb and glanced in the rearview mirror to catch a glimpse of Jane still standing there.

"What are we going to do about those two?" she asked.

"We're not going to do anything," Darla replied, already formulating her plan. "But when we get home, I'm going to rattle Beth's chain."

"You'll never guess who we ran into tonight."

"I don't know," Beth shrugged. "Gwen and Meg."

"Nope. Jane."

Beth looked up at her and Darla smiled. Now she had her attention.

"Where did you see her?"

"Downtown. She was on her way to the bar and she had someone with her."

Beth looked down at her marking again.

"Some woman named Lynn. I've never seen her before."

Beth shrugged. As if she should care.

"And unless the chemotherapy has totally fried my brain, I'd say that Lynn was more with Jane than Jane was with her, if you catch my drift."

Beth looked up at her again.

"She also made a point of asking about you and asking me to tell you she says hello."

"Is there some reason you're doing this?" she snapped. "So Jane's got a new girlfriend. Good for her!"

"Oh. You're right," Darla flippantly agreed. "I only told you as a senseless act of torture. You just go right on back to your marking."

"And what exactly is it you think I should do?"

"Get up off your butt and go after her," she slowly doled out her firm instructions.

"If I called her, she'd probably just hang up again."

"I don't think so."

"Well, I do."

"Then go and see her," Darla pushed. "She can't hang up on you in person."

Beth looked away. Even if she went to see her, she wouldn't know what to say.

Darla leaned down and kissed her on top of the head. "Don't stay up all night driving yourself crazy," she softly advised. "Do something. The only reason I'm pushing is because I know you want to."

Beth dropped her head into her hands. She hated it when Dar was right.

She sat in her car and waited. There was nothing else to do. The concierge had confirmed that Ms. Tolliver did still reside in the building, but she was not in at the moment. Beth glanced at her watch. It was nearly midnight. It was beginning to look like Jane's date had turned into an overnight stay.

Beth perked up at the sudden appearance of her car and then scowled as she watched her pull into the visitor's parking lot. Jane always parked in the underground garage. Either she wasn't alone or she was just planning a short stop at home. Beth scrutinized the car for more evidence. Jane got out and locked her door with the key. Beth smiled. She was home at least for a while and she was definitely on her own. Beth took a deep breath and opened her car door.

"Jane?" she called out to her.

Her head swivelled in Beth's direction. She stood there for a moment or two and then crossed the parking lot.

"Hi there," she smiled. "I thought that was you."

Beth smiled back and leaned against her car, furiously trying to come up with something to say.

"New car?" she inquired.

Beth nodded. Her smile wilted as a car pulled in and parked beside Jane's. It evaporated completely as its lone female occupant got out to coolly observe the goings-on.

"Just coming by to show it off?"

Beth laughed at herself and shook her head. "Actually, I came by to talk, but I see you've got other plans."

Jane's eyes followed Beth's to arrive at her now less-than-patiently waiting guest.

"Perhaps another time?" Beth sadly suggested.

Jane looked back at Lynn and then at Beth again. "You take my keys and go on in. I'll just take a moment to explain."

Beth watched her extract her car key from the case.

"This one's for the front door and this one's for the apartment," she showed her.

Beth stood frozen, staring at Jane's outstretched hand. She looked up for further confirmation.

"Last offer," Jane advised with a smile.

Beth reached out and took the keys.

"I don't know how you can do that," she muttered.

"Do what?"

"Kiss me like that," Darla clarified.

"Like what?"

"Like you want to make love to me."

"I do."

"I wouldn't know why," she grumbled. "I'm old and ugly."

"Oh, come on," Keely cajoled her. "You are not. You're extremely cute and decidedly hot."

"I don't know how you can find me even remotely appealing," she countered. "My hair's falling out by the handful, I've got so many scars on what's left of me that I look like a bloody road map and the inside of my mouth tastes like a goddamned scrap metal heap. I can only imagine what lovely odours and flavours the rest of my body must be emanating."

"Have you heard me complaining?"

"No," she growled. "But you wouldn't. You love me."

"Yes, I do," she readily agreed. "Very much."

Darla yawned and then sighed.

"You're tired," Keely decided, and turned out the light.

Darla rolled over and put her head on Keely's shoulder. Keely closed her eyes, concentrating on lying as still as humanly possible. Darla nuzzled her neck. Keely smiled. Darla licked her behind her ear. Keely promptly took her cue and kissed her like they both wanted her to.

"Did you get a drink?" she asked a moderately uncomfortable-looking Beth.

She smiled and shook her head.

"I'll get you one then," she decided and retreated into the kitchen.

Beth looked around the room. It bordered on almost messy for Jane. The dining-room table was piled with books and the coffee table was littered with file folders. Jane had simply filled the vacant time slots her absence had created with work.

"I'm all out of Scotch," she reluctantly informed her. "Can I get you something else instead? A beer perhaps? Or a glass of wine?"

"Wine might be nice," Beth opted.

Jane reappeared with glasses in hand.

"Thank you," she accepted courteously.

Jane smiled back at her and sank into the safety of her favourite chair. Beth stacked the file folders in front of her to make room on the table for her glass.

"Sorry about the mess," Jane apologized. "I've been working a lot at home these days, and I wasn't expecting any visitors."

Beth smirked at the obvious untruth.

"Ah ... that wasn't planned," she stammered. "It just kind of happened."

Beth tried not to smirk again.

"So how have you been?" she inquired.

"Very well. And you?"

Jane smiled. "Fine."

"You've put on a little weight," Beth observed. "It looks good. You were always too thin."

Jane looked down at herself and then back up at Beth again. "I haven't been running very much lately," she explained.

Beth smiled and picked up her glass of wine.

"Did Dar and Keely mentioned bumping into me tonight?" she switched topics abruptly.

Beth nodded.

"I'm sorry about Dar being ill again. It must have come as quite a shock."

She nodded again. "It came out of nowhere. The tumour showed up on the mammogram she had during her check-up in December. They didn't find any signs of cancer anywhere else in her body, but they still wanted to treat it very aggressively. I can't say as I blame her for refusing to have a second mastectomy. She agreed to a lumpectomy just after Christmas and then radiation, and now the chemotherapy."

"I'm sorry," she repeated.

Beth took a taste of her wine.

"I take it from all appearances tonight that Dar and Keely are still firmly together?"

"Yes," Beth replied. "We were all worried that Keely would fall off the wagon when Dar got sick but she surprised all of us, herself included. She moved into the house right around the time Dar started chemo."

"And how's that arrangement working out?"

"It's nice having her around again," Beth smiled. "Dar's still Dar," she laughed. "And Keely and I are good friends."

Jane nodded at her not-so-subtle clarification. She took a sip of her soda water to fill the latest gap in the conversation.

"I hope your friend in the parking lot wasn't too angry," Beth ventured.

Jane shook her head.

"Is that something serious?"

Jane shrugged. "Not really."

Beth watched her drink from her glass again. "So she doesn't know you're pregnant then?"

Jane coughed and finally managed to swallow.

"I'm sorry," Beth apologized. "Are you okay?"

Jane cleared her throat and nodded.

"You are pregnant, aren't you?"

"Eleven weeks," she confirmed.

Beth smiled. "Congratulations."

"Thank you," she accepted graciously.

Beth looked at her for a moment or two and then set her glass down on the coffee table to get to her feet. Jane rose to follow her to the door, as mystified by the abruptness of her departure as by the bizarreness of the entire visit. Beth picked up her coat and slipped it on.

"It was nice seeing you again," she offered.

"Yes," Jane agreed.

Beth hesitated awkwardly. "We should have dinner sometime," she eventually braved.

"Yes, we should," she concurred.

The silence stretched to an eternity.

"How's tomorrow?" Jane took the giant leap.

Beth smiled. "That would be lovely. What time?"

"Around six-thirty?"

Beth nodded.

"Oh, wait," she reconsidered. "I think I have a late appointment."

Beth was beyond disappointed.

"I'll cancel," Jane decided.

"Shall I meet you at your office, or would you rather I didn't come by there again?"

Jane smiled at the hint of a tease. "I'll see you there then," she beamed.

"Come on, Old Girl," Keely nudged her. "Time to rise and shine."

Darla groaned.

"Come on now," Keely coaxed. "I already let you sleep an extra half hour after the alarm."

She opened her eyes and then closed them again.

"It's almost eight o'clock, Dar. We have to be at the hospital for your treatment at nine."

Darla promptly pulled the covers over her head.

"She's really sick again this time," Beth worried. "I shouldn't have said I'd go."

"It's okay, Beth."

"But what if you need help?"

"Then I'll call Gwen," Keely stood her ground firmly.

"I'm going to call and cancel," Beth decided.

"Like hell you will!" Darla bellowed from the bedroom.

Jane opened the new bottle of Scotch and poured her a drink. She didn't know what to think. They'd chatted amicably over dinner but neither of them had really said anything. When she'd suggested a nightcap at her place, she didn't have a clue what Beth's response would be. Jane viewed her immediate acceptance as a good sign. Of what, she had no idea.

Beth wandered into the kitchen to stand behind her. "Let me help you," she suggested. "A woman in your condition shouldn't be doing this," she teased.

Jane turned to smile at her. "How did you know?"

"What? That you're pregnant?"

She nodded.

"I don't know," she shrugged. "I guess mostly from your face."

"My face?"

Beth nodded. "And your breasts."

Jane twitched uncomfortably. Beth tentatively reached out towards the barely noticeable swelling of her belly.

"May I?"

Jane hesitated and then eventually nodded. Beth smiled when her hand reached its destination. Jane tried very hard not to jump out of her skin.

"Hello, Jane Junior," she bent over to address the unborn child. "My name's Beth. Would you mind terribly much if I made love to your mother?" Beth straightened up to take a good look at Jane's face. "She said she wouldn't mind," she relayed apprehensively. "What does Mama say?"

Jane bit the inside of her lip. "I'm not so sure that's a good idea," she finally decided.

Beth sighed. "I still love you."

"And I love you," she replied. "But our problems aren't going to be resolved by jumping right back into bed. We want some pretty different things."

"I'm not so sure that's true any more," Beth dissented. "I've done a lot of thinking and I hope some growing up too. I'm not afraid of the commitment any more."

Jane scanned her face.

"I love you, and I know I'll love your baby too."

Jane didn't know what to say.

"If two screw-ups like Dar and Keely can manage to work things out and survive everything they have been through, we can too. Please, Jane. Say you'll try again."

"I'm not going to rush into anything," she cautiously warned.

Beth smiled. Slow and steady were her new middle names.

"I'm sick and tired of being sick and tired."

"I know," Keely soothed.

"I don't want to play this game any more," she whined.

"I know that too."

"It's not fair," she pouted.

"No, it isn't," Keely agreed.

"I'm tired."

"Then close your eyes."

Darla did as she was told and then opened them a moment later. "I can't sleep."

"Sure you can."

"No, I can't," she countered. "Every time I close my eyes, all I can think about is puking again."

"Then I'll tell you a story."

"Fat lot of good that will do," she muttered.

"Once upon a time there was this extremely cute sixteen-year-old kid," Keely began.

Darla smiled.

"And she lusted after this beautiful princess ...."

"Who was really a cantankerous old witch ...."

"A cantankerous young witch at that time," Keely corrected.

She smiled again. "Go on."

"The beautiful princess played hard to get and then disappeared for years and years."

Darla yawned.

"And then one day, long after the kid had grown up, they met again in an enchanted place."

Darla's eyelids drifted to half-mast. "And they fell in love."

"That's right," Keely confirmed, pulling the covers up over her shoulders. "And then the princess and the overgrown kid tormented each other for a very long time."

"Until they realized how stupid they were being," she sleepily provided.

"And then they kissed and made up." Keely waited and listened to the evenness of her breathing. "And they lived happily ever after," she wearily finished and closed her eyes.

"I'll call you tomorrow," she offered.

Jane nodded and yawned again.

"Get some sleep, you two."

Jane smiled sleepily. Beth reached out and touched the side of her face.

"I'd really very much like to kiss you," she expressed her fondest desire. "May I?"

Jane's mouth met hers more than halfway.

"Oh, I'm sorry," she apologized and turned off the overhead light immediately.

"It's okay, Beth. You can turn the light on again."

She sat down opposite her at the table instead. "Rough night?" she guessed.

Keely nodded and wiped her tears on her sleeve.

"Sometimes I wonder if we did the right thing by pushing her into chemotherapy."

"I know you do," she consoled her. "Me too."

"She was sick as a dog all night again."

Beth reached across the table and took her hand. She wished there was something she could say or do.

"So how did it go with you?"

Beth shrugged. "I really don't know. She wants to take things slow."

Keely nodded distractedly.

"I did manage to wheedle a kiss good night though."

Keely smiled. She didn't know what she'd do without her. Either of them.

"Everything will be fine," she reassured herself as much as Keely. "You'll see."

"Did Beth go out with Jane again?"

Keely nodded. "She went over for a cup of tea."

"Cup of tea, my ass," Darla chuckled. "She's on a mission to get laid."

Keely laughed.

"She is," Darla stated with certainty. "Trust me."

Keely sat gingerly on the side of the bed. "Can I get you anything?" she checked.

"How about a good night's sleep? Or a new body?" she added sarcastically. "And while you're at it, how about a right breast or at least a left one without a scar on it?"

Keely sighed. "I wish I could," she replied. "More than anything."

It was just supposed to have been a good-night kiss. The moment their lips met, Jane knew she was in way over her head. She gave up any further illusion of control and wrapped her arms around her. So much for taking things slow. Beth's tongue greeted hers warmly. Jane backed off a step.

"Oh god," Beth groaned. "Don't say no."

"I wasn't going to," she grinned. "I was just going to suggest we take this into the bedroom."

She sat bolt upright in bed. "Keely?" she panicked.

"I'm here," she reached out and took her hand.

Darla lay back down again. Her heart was pounding and she was covered with sweat.

"It's okay," Keely comforted her. "It was just a bad dream."

Darla took a deep breath. Her stomach flip-flopped and rumbled loudly.

"Are you hungry?"

"I don't know what I am," she moped dejectedly.

"Why don't I make you something to eat? Sometimes it helps settle your stomach," she suggested optimistically.

Darla put her head on Keely's shoulder. "Maybe in a bit. Right now could you just hold me?"

Keely put her arms around her and held on for dear life.

"Uh-uh," she feebly protested as Beth's tongue began encouraging her again. "No, really," she assured her. "You've done me in."

Beth propped herself on her elbow to take a good look at her. "Are you okay?"

Jane smiled contentedly and nodded.

"Then what gives? Once is never enough for you."

"I'm tired," Jane explained.

Beth lay her sticky thigh over Jane's two and snuggled in beside her. "I suppose you are orgasming for two," she considered.

Jane chuckled. Beth kissed her on the side of the neck. Jane sighed and closed her eyes. Beth's hand crept across her chest. Her fingers brought Jane's drowsy nipple back to life instantly.

"Was that the first time Jane Junior's gone for a test drive?"

Jane's eyes popped open.

"Never mind," she chastised herself. "That's none of my business."

Jane kissed her on the top of the head and closed her eyes again. Beth's lips replaced her hand. Jane swallowed as Beth devoured her breast. She moaned when Beth's hand hit the warm target of its slow descent.

Beth slid down the bed. Jane groaned as Beth's tongue reached out to taste her and then plunged inside her. She buried her hands in her lover's hair as Beth's fingers filled the depth of her desire. Jane's silky walls turned to corduroy and her grip tightened on the back of Beth's head. Beth slowed her tongue's pace to drink every ounce of her Jane's ecstasy in. She eased her caresses to the point of stillness and lay her cheek against the wet, matted curls to enjoy the sweet sensation of feeling Jane's slowing pulse from deep inside her.

"I love you," she told her Jane.

"I love you too. And the answer to your question is yes," she put it to rest. "Tonight was Jane Junior's first test drive. I haven't made love with anyone since the last time with you."

Darla removed the washcloth tentatively. Much to her relief, her nose had stopped bleeding. There was no need to wake Keely. She shifted down onto the pillows again to watch her sleep. Keely was so exhausted these days her skin looked almost as grey as her own. Her cancer was killing Keely too.

She reached up to the chain around her neck and toyed with the ring that no longer fit her bloated finger. Keely had given it to her the day she'd found out she had cancer again. Waiting until Christmas had seemed inconceivable. She'd had it made to match the one she'd received on her birthday. The inscription even read "Love always, Keely." A tear trickled down her left cheek. Always was supposed to be a long time.

Keely answered the door but not before she'd pounded for a second time.

"Where's Beth?" she angrily demanded.

Keely put her hand on Jane's shoulder and backed her out the door, pulling it closed behind them.

"I want to see Beth!" she asserted again.

"Look, Jane. I don't know what the hell your problem is, but this household doesn't need this sort of crap right now! Okay?"

"Sorry," she eased off a bit. "But I really need to see Beth."

"Can't it wait until morning? Dar's sleeping, or at least she was."

Jane sighed in frustration. "I'm sorry," she apologized again. "I didn't think."

"You're right. You didn't," Keely agreed.

The door opened behind them.

"What's going on?"

"Oh, shit," Jane swore at the entire situation. "I'm sorry I woke you."

"What's going on?" Darla emphatically repeated.

"Jane wants to see Beth," Keely explained.

"So let her," Darla shrugged and held the door for everyone to come in.

Jane headed immediately towards the stairs.

"I'm not so sure about this," Keely wavered. "She's really mad."

"Oh come on, Old Girl," Darla cajoled her. "Don't be such a stick in the mud. Let the kids kiss and make up. I'm taking you back to bed."

"Keely?" the commotion brought Beth to wakefulness. "What's wrong? Is Dar sick again?"

"It's not Keely," came the familiar voice in the darkness. "It's your other ex-lover."

Beth zeroed in on the ex part. Jane was clearly furious. "Oh, Louise," she attempted to disarm her.

"Very fucking funny!"

Beth sat up. Jane had used the F word. A very uncommon thing.

"What the fuck's going on? I woke up and you were gone."

"I left you a note ...."

"Great note!" she flew off the handle. "Sorry I had to leave. Thanks for tonight. Love, Beth?" Jane tossed the offending piece of paper on the bed. "What the fuck is thanks for tonight supposed to mean? Why didn't you just put thanks for the sex?"

"Jane, I ...."

"I thought we were through playing games," she ranted. "I thought you were ready to make a commitment?"

"I am. It's just that I was really worried about Dar ...."

"Oh Christ!" she seethed. "So worried you couldn't

even stay one night?"

Beth fell silent. This wasn't at all what she had planned. They were supposed to make love, make up and walk off into the sunset hand in hand.

"If you're so ready to make a commitment, then when are you going to move in with me?"

Beth looked away.

"So, what?" Jane laughed bitterly. "It goes back to the way it was before? Except now it's okay with you if I have a baby?"

"I do want to be with you but ...."

"But still only on a part-time basis," she cut her off. "That's all I'll ever be to you, part-time Jane."

"I can't go now," she tried to explain. "Dar and Keely ...."

"Forget it!" she snapped. "I get the picture. They'll always be more important to you!"

"Jane, please. Listen to me."

She shook her head. "I've heard more than enough empty promises from you. Good-bye, Beth."

"Jane, wait!"

She ignored her completely. Jane took the stairs two at time, anxious to be anywhere but there.

"Not leaving us so soon are you, counsellor?" she intervened.

Jane paused momentarily.

"And it doesn't look like a very happy exit either," she observed drily.

Jane continued on into the living room. An ugly encounter with Dar was something she just didn't need.

"I suppose you're angry with Beth because she won't move in with you. I guess you've got me to thank for that. It's really got nothing to do with you."

Jane turned around to face her. "Make your point, Dar. I haven't got all night."

"Beth won't move in with you because she thinks Keely and I need her here, and the truth of the matter is that for the next little while we do," she laid it on the line. "She loves you and very much needs you right now. She thinks I'm going to die. Most of the time Keely does too."

Jane sank into a nearby chair, defeated and defused.

"Well, I've said what I wanted to say," Darla concluded. "Do with it what you will. Now if you'll excuse me, I don't seem to be feeling very well."

Beth sat up and dried her eyes when she heard her in the bathroom again. "It's okay, Keely," she answered the footsteps on the stairs. "I'm coming."

"It's not Keely," she replied. "It's 'Louise' again."

Beth reached for her robe. "Is Dar alone?"

Jane shook her head. "Keely's up with her."

Beth hesitated and then put her robe down again.

"You go if you want to," Jane advised. "I'll wait."

"She'll let me know if she needs me," she declined.

Jane sat wearily on the edge of the bed. "I'm sorry," were the only words she could think of to say.

Beth nodded. "I am, too. I was afraid you'd left."

"Your friend Dar had an enlightening little chat with me on her way to the bathroom."

Beth smiled at Dar's overt meddling.

"I wish you'd told me."

"I wish you had let me."

Jane nodded. She did too.

"They're not more important to me than you. Do you know that?"

"I always felt like they were."

"And I always felt like you were expecting me to choose."

Jane turned to look at her.

"I love both of them," she openly admitted. "But I also love you."

Jane looked at the wall on the far side of the room. "The running back and forth makes me crazy."

"So what do you want to do?"

Jane shrugged. She didn't have a clue.

"You could stay here with me for a while."

Jane laughed. There was crazy and then there was insane. She bit the inside of her lip and stared at her hands. They were at an impasse again.

"So I guess this is it then," Beth recognized the signs. "I wish it could be different," she whispered softly.

Jane nodded. "Me too."

"Then stay," Beth managed to find her voice to say.

"Ah, shit," she sighed. "You wear me out."

"Does that mean Jane and Beth and baby will make three?" she broached hopefully.

Jane laughed at the absurdity. "And Aunt Dar and Aunt Keely make it four and five?"

"Something like that," Beth readily agreed.

Jane kicked her shoes off and lay down beside her. "What the hell?" she gave in to the insanity. "It all seems like a perfectly rational plan to me."

June

"WHEN WAS THE last time we made love?"

Keely popped the last corner of the fitted sheet on. "I don't know," she shrugged. "A little while ago."

"We haven't made love in weeks. Not since April fourteenth."

Keely smiled and shook the pillow into its case. "You're sure about that now, are you?"

Darla nodded. "I figured it out yesterday."

"We'll have to make up for lost time as soon as you're feeling better then, won't we?" she returned lightly. "Now back into bed with you, Old Girl," she directed.

Darla hoisted herself out of the chair and sat on the edge of the bed. Feeling better was still light years away, and time was slipping through her fingers with each passing day.

"I made the official announcement at work today."

"And?"

"And I got two congratulations and several shocked and appalled looks," Jane snickered. "I think they all thought I was a lesbian."

Beth chuckled too.

"But they were less than amused by my request to go to a four-day work week."

"Will they give it to you?"

Jane smiled. "They have to. If they don't, I'll quit and do the stay-at-home mom thing."

Beth just shook her head. Pregnancy was doing some strange things to her Jane. From Ms. Workaholic LL B to Mama Homebody in just twenty weeks.

"Of course, if that happens you'll have to make an honest woman out of me and marry me."

"I thought we already were," Beth returned playfully.

Jane grinned. "I was hoping you'd see it that way. The staff picnic's on Sunday and we're supposed to bring our spouses."

"I need to ask you a favour."

Jane looked at her expectantly.

"And you have to promise not to tell Keely. Or Beth either," she further stipulated.

"Okay," she agreed reluctantly.

Darla extended the piece of paper. Jane read it over and then silently set it on the table between them.

"You don't have to if you don't want to."

"No, it's not that," she replied. "I haven't handled many wills, that's all."

Darla nodded.

"And I probably shouldn't do it anyway. Beth is listed as one of your beneficiaries," she pointed out.

Darla sighed and nodded again.

"Why are you doing this now?"

Darla shrugged. "It's just time."

Jane didn't like the way things added up. Not at all.

"Relax, Jane," she answered the worried look on her face. "I'm not planning on killing myself, if that's what you're thinking. At least not overtly," she qualified. "I've decided to stop the chemotherapy."

Her announcement didn't exactly take Jane by surprise.

"I haven't told Keely yet. Or Beth either," she clarified. "I thought I'd wait until the weekend."

Jane nodded and picked up the piece of paper again. "I'm having lunch with my dad today," she relayed. "Pete's done lots of wills. I'll ask him to look it over and call you. I'm sure he can arrange to drop by sometime when Keely's at work."

Darla smiled at her. "Thanks, Jane. You're a good friend."

Beth topped up their coffee cups. "There's more wrong than just the usual," she decided.

"Dar's really depressed," Keely worried. "Even on the few days when she's feeling okay, she doesn't bother to get dressed and she never laughs any more."

Beth nodded. She'd noticed too.

"And she's getting along with everybody. Even Brock."

Beth smiled. "Jane said she was bitchy with her on Monday."

"Oh, yeah?" Keely brightened.

"I guess she didn't much care for Jane getting up with her when she was sick in the night."

Keely scowled. "I didn't hear her."

"Neither did I. And I guess it's not the first time either. From the little that Jane said, I gather they've had more than a few late-night conversations."

Keely looked at her blankly.

Beth shrugged. "I didn't know either."

Brock hustled out the door as soon as he spotted the white Mercedes. Something had to be really wrong for Darla to have driven over by herself.

"Hi," he greeted her pleasantly. "What brings you by?"

Darla smiled at him through the open window. "I thought I'd just stop in on my way home from the doctor's."

"My good-looking twin sister's having lunch with her favourite sister-in-law," he kept things decidedly light. "Want me to call her and tell her you're here?"

Darla shook her head. "Actually, I came by to talk to you."

He had a bad feeling he knew what about too.

"Can you spare a few minutes?"

Brock nodded and got in the car.

"So it's kind of like the flu?"

Keely nodded. "She's got it all the time lately. Last night she had a temperature of 102."

Cindy set her burger back on her plate. "Is there anything I can do?"

Keely shook her head. "Beth helps out a lot and Jane too."

Cindy smiled. "I meant for you."

Keely shook her head again. Cindy got up from the table.

"Coffee?" she offered.

"I'd rather have a beer," Keely answered honestly.

"Absolutely not," she refused flatly.

Keely didn't say anything.

"Tea?" she tried again.

"How about a cigarette?" Keely suggested instead.

Cindy regrouped for attempt number three. "If you don't want coffee or tea, how about me?"

Keely managed to force out a smile.

"Does Keely know yet?"

She shook her head. "Brock and Jane do, and now you."

"You told Brock and Jane before me? And me before Keely?"

Darla nodded. "I wanted you to have someone to talk to who already knew, and I also wanted to be sure that everybody would be over their initial reaction enough to be there for Keely."

Beth saw the logic but was still less than impressed.

"I'm sorry if the way I chose to do things upsets you."

Beth sighed.

"Forgive me?"

She nodded.

"For stopping treatment too?"

Beth smiled and nodded again. It was the hardest thing she'd ever had to do.

Gwen mutely nodded. There really wasn't much to say. She'd been expecting the announcement for days.

"So how are you feeling about it?"

Keely shrugged. "I guess in a way I understand. She's had every possible rotten side effect going, and they really did try everything they could but ...."

Gwen nodded. The sentence really didn't require completion.

"It's just hard," Keely abridged. "For everybody."

Gwen screwed up her face. "How on earth am I going to tell Theron? He worships the ground Dar walks on. He's going to be really upset."

"Dar's going to tell him herself when he stops by after school today."

"Is he still coming by every day?"

Keely nodded. "He's been there every day since she got

out of the hospital after her lumpectomy in January. Some days she was too sick to see him, and sometimes he'd just sit there while she slept, but most of the time they'd get at least a little visit in."

Gwen smiled. "He's quite a kid."

Keely nodded at her understatement. "That he is."

"Does this mean Keely's going to start smoking again?"

Darla looked at him blankly.

"She said she'd quit smoking if you did chemotherapy," Theron reminded her.

Darla smiled. "No, I don't think so."

"Oh," he said and then just stood there.

"Why don't you sit down beside me?"

He shook his head and wandered over to stare out the window instead. Darla got up off the sofa and came up behind him.

"It's stupid to cry," he moaned.

"No, it's not. Sometimes it's the best thing you can do."

Theron chewed on the inside of his lip. "Are you going to die?"

"Someday, yes. But not right away."

"Will you get cancer again?"

"I really don't know."

"Do the doctors think so?"

"They really don't know either."

Theron heaved a thunderous sigh.

"I won't feel so sick all the time now," she tried.

He didn't say anything.

"And we'll be able to do things again."

"Like take the Harley for a ride?"

Darla smiled. "Not right away. But maybe later in the summer," she suggested hopefully.

Theron sniffled and wiped his nose on his sleeve. "I don't want you to die."

Darla put her arm around him. "Come here for a hug, big guy."

"I think the party surprised Keely completely, don't you?"

Beth nodded.

"Everybody seemed to have a good time," Jane rambled on. "It sure beat last week's barbeque."

Beth halfheartedly smiled.

"I got to know both Brock and Cindy a little better and Gwen too."

Beth finished undressing and crawled into bed.

"Has Meg always been that quiet?"

"I don't know her very well," she replied. "From what Keely says, I guess so."

Jane turned out the light. "Theron sure had a great time with the camera, didn't he?"

Beth put her head on her shoulder. Jane wrapped her arms around her and held on tight. The tears were bound to come eventually. It had been one very long week.

Keely sank down on the edge of the bed. She braved opening the photo album.

"Brock dug up the old pictures of you, and I managed to find a few of me that were taken around the time we met. You were pretty cute at sixteen," she teased.

Keely flipped to page two.

"That picture of us dates back to right around the time of your twenty-sixth birthday. We set the timer on the camera, remember?"

Keely smiled.

"All of the pictures of us renovating this place were easy to come up with. I think there must be about a hundred more down in my office."

Keely silently poured over the collection.

"Probably some of those are out of order," Darla remarked on the next section. "They span the next five years or so. I know you took this picture of me on my forty-second birthday," she pointed out. "And this one is from New Year's 1983. You were really mad at me because I made you go out. Remember?"

Keely nodded and turned the page.

"Christmas 1987, the year the three of us lived together," she continued her running commentary. "We were eating turkey for weeks. And those were taken at the cottage last summer. There really weren't many taken since then. That's why Theron was running around with the Polaroid tonight. I asked him not to take any pictures of me though. There will be plenty of time for that when I'm looking like myself again. The blank pages at the end are intentional," she explained. "We'll fill them up over the next twenty-four years or so."

Keely closed the album cover and lay down to put her head in Darla's lap. She'd been crying since page three.

"At least we didn't fight on your birthday this year," she attempted some levity.

Keely managed to smile like she was supposed to.

"Happy fortieth birthday, Keely," she wished her. "I love you."

August

"HELLO, HANDSOME," she greeted him.

"Hi ya, sexy," Brock replied. "Nice hat."

Darla returned his smile.

"So what can I do for you?"

"A couple of favours?" she suggested hopefully.

"Anything for you," he bantered easily.

"Can I steal your sister for a week? Jane's invited us to join them at her father's cottage, and Keely's too guilty to ask for a vacation after all the time she took off to play nursemaid to me. I know it's a lot to ask, but we could both really stand the holiday."

"No problem," he agreed immediately.

She kissed him on the cheek. "Thank you."

Brock smiled at her awkwardly. "And the other favour?" he broached.

"Is business related. Can you quote a job for me?"

"Are you sure you don't mind them coming along?"

Jane smiled. "If I minded would I have invited them?" she asked rhetorically.

Beth watched her travel from the dresser back to the suitcase again. If she didn't know better, she'd think she was up to something.

"Not again," she groaned.

Darla looked up.

"Dildos must be in vogue," Beth muttered in disgust. "This is the third girl-meets-girl story in a row where they spend more time going on about so-and-so's dildo than anything else."

Darla chuckled and went back to her own book. There were no dildos in it. Not yet anyway.

"Have you ever used one?"

Darla smiled but didn't say anything.

"Stupid question," she drew her own conclusion.

"Haven't you?"

"No. And I don't want to either."

Darla returned her attention to the page in front of her again. Beth watched her for a moment or two, and when it was clear the topic had been dropped, closed her eyes to enjoy the afternoon sun.

"I must remember to buy Jane a strap-on for Christmas," Darla remarked ever so innocently.

Beth's aim was off. Her book missed Darla's head by a good foot.

"I'm sorry," she apologized. "I didn't mean to wake you. You looked cold so I thought I should cover you up."

Jane yawned. "It's okay, Keely. I wasn't really asleep anyway. I was just kind of drifting." She heaved herself upright on the sofa. "Are the other two still on the beach?"

Keely nodded and sat down beside her. "Knowing those sun bunnies, that's where they will be spending the week."

Jane stretched lazily. "Oh," she jumped and brought her hand to her tummy.

"What's the matter?"

"Nothing," Jane smiled. "Jane Junior's awake now too."

"Would it be okay if I felt her moving?" she asked hesitantly.

Her request surprised Jane completely. Keely had never expressed any interest before. She picked up Keely's hand and placed it on her rounded belly. Keely's face lit up immediately. Jane was elated with her accomplishment. Getting a smile out of Keely these days was anything but easy.

"Keely?" she nudged her. "Keely?"

She sat bolt upright in bed, instantly awake. "What's wrong?"

"Feel this."

"Where?"

Darla grabbed her hand and brought it to the back of her head. "Is that what I think it is?"

"Where?"

"All over the back of my head," she beamed.

Keely's heart rate dropped significantly. There wasn't another lump. There was just soft peach fuzz that was promising to grow into hair.

"Isn't it great?" she celebrated.

"It sure is," Keely quietly agreed.

Jane made what felt like her hundredth return trip from the bathroom that night. She stopped short. The cottage door was open and it hadn't been earlier. Keely was sitting on the steps of the deck, looking out over the lake. Jane stood by helplessly and watched her cry. Keely turned in her direction and then immediately looked away again. Jane approached her cautiously.

"Can I help?"

Keely shook her head.

"Do you want me to get Dar or Beth for you?"

Keely shook her head again. What she really wanted was a cigarette. She wiped her face on the sleeve of her sweatshirt. Jane sat down beside her.

"I'm not sure I'd be really comfortable if you caught me falling apart either," she remarked. "Sometimes it feels like we don't know each other very well."

Keely smiled at her diplomacy.

"I'm a good listener," she offered hopefully.

Keely looked back out over the lake. "Dar's hair's growing back."

Jane smiled.

"She woke me up a little while ago to show me." Keely looked away as the tears came again. "I thought she'd found another lump," she struggled to explain.

Jane waited patiently for her to regain her composure again.

"She was all excited about it," Keely relayed. "She's so anxious for everything to get back to normal, and I'm just scared shitless that's never going to happen."

"It's hard to pretend everything's okay when it doesn't feel that way," Jane commiserated. "I know it's not at all the same, but last fall when Beth and I split up, I turned into a blubbering basket case. It was so bad I even moved in with Pete for a while. But nobody at work knew. I can't imagine pretending twenty-four hours a day."

"Every time she coughs or has an ache or pain I nearly go insane." Keely fought off her tears again. "The fear is there constantly."

Jane nodded sympathetically. "I'm sure it must be."

"I know she feels okay right now," Keely acknowledged. "But she did last fall too. And even if the cancer doesn't come back this year, what about next year or the year after that?"

Jane put her hand on Keely's arm. There were no words to say.

Keely looked down at her feet. "Dar's always been really good at living for today, but I don't know how to. I never have. If she gets sick again, I'll never be able to forgive myself for not fighting her decision to stop the chemotherapy."

Jane thought long and hard about what to say. "Beth doesn't think she'll get sick again and for whatever it's worth, I don't either," she offered quietly. "Tomorrow has an interesting way of turning into today, Keely. And today always becomes yesterday," she reinforced positively. "Twenty years from now we'll be sitting here, trying to figure out what all the fuss was about. And Jane Junior will probably be chasing after her Aunt Dar, struggling to keep up."

Keely looked directly at her for the first time. "Do you really think so?"

Jane nodded. "I honestly do."

Keely looked back out over the lake again. More than anything she wished she could find a way to start believing it too.

Beth yawned and adjusted her angle to the sun.

"Did Jane keep you up half the night again?"

"Pregnancy has some desirable side effects," she grinned happily.

Darla's smile faded. "Keely and I haven't made love since April," she mourned woefully.

Beth's jaw dropped. She had no idea.

"Who would want to make love with someone as old and ugly as me?"

"Keely," she answered with certainty.

Darla shook her head. "She's so used to me being tired or pukey that she's probably given up the notion completely, and I just don't know how any more."

"It's easy," Beth teased. "You start out by kissing her and then you say I love you. And if that doesn't work, you hit her with a verbal two-by-four. Something subtle like, Hey baby. Want to sit on my face?"

Darla laughed hysterically. Beth was proud of herself. It was the most wonderful sound she'd heard in weeks.

"Good night," Keely wished her.

Darla propped herself up on an elbow and kissed Keely pointedly. Keely's tongue greeted hers warmly. Darla kissed her again and Keely returned it, but then seemed quite content to just let things be. Disappointed, Darla lay back down again.

"I love you," she said.

Keely smiled sleepily. "I love you too."

Darla opened her mouth, but no matter how hard she tried, Beth's verbal two-by-four just wouldn't come out. She mentally rephrased it a thousand ways. "Make love to me," she at long last braved.

Keely didn't say or do anything. Darla sighed. She'd taken too long. Keely had fallen asleep.

Beth knew she had to. She'd put it off for as long as she could. She'd promised herself weeks ago that if the much-avoided topic hadn't been dealt with before, she'd bring it up herself while they were on holidays. She summoned all her courage. It was now or never.

"I suppose when we get back we should think about moving," she broached the issue casually.

Jane buried her face in Beth's breasts. "Mmm," was all she said.

"I'm sure you're anxious to get back into your own place."

Jane tickled her nipple with her lips. "We can't move back into the condo," she replied dreamily. "I sold it last week."

"You did?"

"Uh-huh," Jane slurped out as she traced a line to Beth's other nipple with her tongue.

"So you still want to move somewhere bigger," she concluded.

"Bigger?" she considered. "Not really."

Beth intercepted Jane's hand as it travelled up her thigh. "Are you going to tell me what's going on?"

Jane smiled. She was having a good time.

"Are we moving or not?" her blood pressure crept up.

It was time to fess up. "We're moving," she confirmed.

Beth's heart sank. Jane was sticking to her guns.

"Just not very far," she added mischievously. "Dar's drawn up some renovation plans for the main floor."

It took a moment for the words to sink in.

"She's decided to retire," Jane explained. "She offered us her office space."

Beth was elated and then immediately guilty. "You're only doing this for me. Living there makes you crazy."

"It used to," Jane conceded. "I'm an only child," she smiled. "It just took me a while to get used to living in a larger family."

"You're really sure about this, aren't you?"

Darla nodded. She was positive.

"Don't you think you're going to be bored?"

"Not in the least," she dismissed the possibility.

"I wish you'd waited until you were feeling better to decide," Keely resisted. "Once you renovate your office space, it's kind of too late to change your mind."

"I'm not going to change my mind. And besides, I'll set up the guest bedroom as a little office. I'll still take on the odd job from time to time, and if I get bored I'll just do a little more."

Keely was less than convinced.

"I told you last summer that I was planning on retiring in the next couple of years anyway," Darla reminded her.

"As I recall, you also said you were going to build a new house for your retirement. What happened to that idea?"

Darla smiled. "That old house is too much part of us to leave behind. I realized I couldn't imagine living anywhere but there. Can you?"

"Not really," Keely conceded.

Darla watched the wheels turning. Keely was very busy thinking.

"You don't have to hire anybody," she gave in to the plan reluctantly. "I'll do it in my spare time."

"Like hell you will," Darla grinned. "I'm going to keep you far too busy for that sort of thing. We'll do just enough that it's not work, but still get to have some fun."

Keely scowled. "You'll end up overdoing it. I know you."

"No, I won't," she promised and leaned over to give her a little kiss. "I love you," she said.

Keely shook her head at the whole thing and crawled out of bed. There was no point in arguing. Dar had made up her mind.

"Keely?"

"All right already," she laughed. "I give in. Do what you want."

Darla sighed. Keely's abrupt departure from between the sheets had already eliminated even the remote possibility.

"Dar's sure in ugly humour today. What's her problem anyway?"

"She's horny," Beth snickered.

"Then why did she offer to do the grocery shopping? We could have done it and given them some time alone."

Beth laughed at the confused look on Jane's face.

"Is Keely playing hard to get?" she asked in disbelief.

Beth shook her head.

"What, then?"

Beth grinned. "Since we're alone and it's such a long story, I think I should tell you in bed."

"What the hell was that back at the store?" Darla muttered. "You cruised every damned woman in the place."

"I was just browsing," she replied lightly.

Darla crossed her arms in a huff. "Looked more like serious shopping to me."

Keely glanced over at her and then looked back at the road ahead again. "I've always looked, Dar," she reacted calmly. "You know that. It's never bothered you before."

"Well, it bothers me now," she snapped and snarled. "It bothers the shit out of me!"

Keely tried really hard not to smile at her rampant case of jealousy.

"And that bimbette back at the corner!" she seethed angrily. "What exactly was the appeal with her? Was it the skirt she was barely wearing or the fact that she might have been all of seventeen?"

Keely's grip slipped and a tiny smile escaped her lips.

"Oh, yeah! You think it's funny. I'm being serious here. I want to know!"

"It was both," Keely jibed her. "You know how I like nubile young things."

Darla shot her a look. "Pull over," she demanded.

Keely reassessed the seriousness of the situation immediately.

"Pull over!" she commanded.

Keely eased the Mercedes onto the shoulder.

"Shut the car off."

She did as she was told obediently.

"Keely, if you don't make love to me right this second, I think I'm going to explode."

Beth got to her feet to help her unpack the groceries. "Where's Dar?"

"In the car."

"What's she doing there?"

"Practising her driving, I hope," Keely growled. "She damned near killed me on the way home."

The door banged shut behind them. "I heard that!"

Beth smiled. They were arguing. Things really were getting back to normal again. She finished unpacking the first bag and reached into the second to lift out the soggy carton. Darla suppressed a giggle. Keely out-and-out laughed.

"What happened to the ice cream?" Beth asked innocently.

"We were tied up for a little while on the way back," Darla beamed.

Beth dropped the melted soup into the sink and stared pointedly at Keely's wrist. "Funny," she remarked devilishly. "I don't see any evidence of rope burns."

Jane lay in bed listening to their crazy laughing, smiling all the while. They really were one twisted family.

"What's the matter?"

"I don't know," Darla shrugged uncomfortably. "I just feel all clumsy."

"You certainly weren't that way in the car," Keely teased.

"No," she laughed. "But now I can't seem to figure out where all the noses go."

"They go anywhere we want them to," she grinned and ducked under the sheet playfully. "And lots of places they're not supposed to go," she demonstrated happily.

"It's only nine-thirty," Beth made note of the time. "Shopping must have been really tiring."

Jane looked in the direction of their bedroom and then back at Beth again. By the sound of things, they weren't exactly sleeping.

Beth burst out laughing. "Quiet sex never was exactly Dar's forte."

Jane smiled. "Shall we go for a walk and give the love-birds a little privacy?"

Keely spooned in behind her and nuzzled her neck. Darla smiled and closed her eyes. Keely licked and nosed at her ear. Darla squirmed at the tickle.

"Again?" she suspected.

"And again and again and again," Keely confirmed.

Darla laughed. Beth hesitated at the sound and then knocked on the door reluctantly.

"Dar?" she called.

"Go away," they responded in unison.

Beth winced. She really hated to interrupt but she had to. "Theron's here to see you."

Darla was still knotting her robe when she opened the door. "Where?"

"In the living room. I think he's upset."

"What about?"

Beth shrugged. "He doesn't seem to want to talk to me."

Darla nodded and approached Theron cautiously. "Hi, big guy. What are you doing here?"

"I came to see you," he answered matter-of-factly.

"How did you get here?"

"I thumbed," he grinned impishly.

Darla rolled her eyes.

"It's no big deal," he cut her off. "I do it all the time."

She was about to get into it with him and then reconsidered. There would be plenty of time for that later. "Does Gwen know you're here?"

He shook his head.

"Okay, Theron. Out with it. What's going on?"

He scanned the floor at his feet.

"Theron? What's wrong?"

"Everything," he whimpered. "Gwen and Meg are moving in together."

"Did you get Theron settled in?"

"What are you doing still awake?" Beth chided her.

Jane rolled onto her back and yawned. "So? What happened?"

"Dar made him call both Gwen and Brock on the car phone," she recounted. "Gwen was really upset about him taking off and Brock was pretty ticked with him for skipping out on work, but in the end they both said he could stay a couple of days."

Jane stretched her arms over her head and then rearranged her positioning again.

"Are you two okay?" Beth checked.

"I'm just having a hard time getting comfortable tonight, that's all."

Images of premature labour danced in Beth's head. "Are you sure?" she double-checked.

"Relax," Jane laughed. "We're both fine."

Beth kissed first one and then the other and curled up beside them for the night.

Keely kept to the water's edge. She was afraid Dar would get too tired if they walked through the deep sand.

"It's probably a terrible thing to say," Darla relayed, "but I'm kind of looking forward to Beth and Jane moving downstairs. It will be nice to have the place just to ourselves again."

"We've never lived together without Beth there," Keely pointed out.

"I was thinking more of how it used to be before then," Darla grinned wickedly. "I can accost you in front of the fire again."

Keely laughed. She was also looking forward to it.

"Do you think it was a mistake to say Theron could stay a couple of days?" she shifted the topic.

Keely shook her head. "A little holiday will probably do him good."

Darla smiled. "It's certainly been good for us. It's made me feel close to you again. The last little while you've felt a million miles away."

"It's felt like that to me too," Keely acknowledged.

Darla slipped her arm through Keely's and leaned against her shoulder.

"Tired?" Keely guessed.

Darla shook her head.

"What then?"

Darla debated. "You'll think it's silly," she decided.

"No, I won't," she promised. "Tell me."

"I think I'm falling in love with you again," she confessed ever so quietly.

Keely smiled. "It's more like still for me."

"I'm sorry, Theron. But Jane's dad's stuff is too big and everybody else's is too small, unless you're willing to consider a pair of Jane's maternity shorts as an option?"

Theron screwed up his face.

"Then you're just going to have to wait until they get back from their walk."

"She won't mind," he whined. "Really."

"That may be," Beth conceded. "But I'm not giving you a pair of Keely's shorts until she says it's okay."

Theron plunked down on the sand. "It's a million degrees and I'm at the beach and I can't go swimming," he got into his feeling-sorry-for-himself routine.

"If you're so hot, why don't you just swim in your underwear?"

Theron squinted at her and then grinned. "I'm not wearing any."

"When does the deal on the condo close?" Keely inquired.

"The first week in November," Jane provided.

"Brock thinks if they put a rush on, the renovations

will take four to six weeks," Darla illuminated. "So you should be able to move in about a week or two before the baby's born."

Theron's ears perked up. "You're moving?"

Beth nodded. "Just downstairs though."

"Oh," he said and stared back into the fire again.

Jane rearranged her head in Beth's lap. "Jane Junior's kicking up a storm again."

All eyes focused on her immediately.

"Why do you call the baby that?" Theron asked.

"I don't know," Jane shrugged. "It's just a nickname."

Theron thought for a moment or two. "How do you know she isn't going to be a he?"

Blank looks flew around the room. Not one of the four had even considered that possibility.

Jane crawled out from under Beth's arm and shuffled into the kitchen mid-yawn. Darla's attention didn't waver from the dishes in the sink. Jane didn't like the look of things.

"Is Keely up yet?" she opened the conversation neutrally.

Darla nodded. "She went fishing with Theron a little while ago."

Jane sat down at the kitchen table. She could tell from her voice that she'd been crying.

"Is everything okay?" she asked unnecessarily.

Darla turned around to face her and attempted a smile. "Everything's fine," she lied.

"No, it's not," she called her bluff. "Now why don't you tell me what's wrong."

Darla took a shaky deep breath. Sooner or later she'd find out anyway.

"You've got some nerve, Mister," Keely made her feelings abundantly clear. "How could you even ask such a thing? You know how sick Dar's been, and what about Gwen? How do you think it would make her feel?"

Theron took his lumps quietly.

"You can't expect everybody to just rearrange their lives to suit you."

"I'm not asking you to. I just thought that since Beth and Jane were moving anyway, and since Meg hates me, maybe I could live with you. That's all."

"Meg doesn't hate you."

"She does too," he countered. "I'm just in the way."

Keely sat down on the log beside him. Theron reached into his pocket and extracted a pack of cigarettes. Keely shot him a look. He ignored her completely and lit one anyway.

"If you're going to be such a rotten little shit, you'd better give me one too."

Theron smiled. All hope was not lost. At least not yet.

"What did Keely say?"

"Nothing," Darla reported. "She just got that panicked look on her face. Not her 'Oh my god, you've got cancer again' expression. More like her 'you're really going to insist on driving, aren't you?' face."

Jane smiled.

"I can't just let him move in," she told herself as much as Jane. "Keely was so looking forward to it being just the two of us again."

Jane nodded.

"What should I do?"

"Talk to Keely, talk to Gwen and talk to Theron," she suggested.

Darla smiled at her forever rational friend.

"Are you and Jane still taking that course on babies?"

"The prenatal classes you mean?"

Theron nodded.

"We've still got four weeks to go."

He picked up a handful of sand. "Do the people there think it's weird because it's two women?" he asked.

Beth smiled. "Some do, but mostly they pretty much ignore us."

Theron opened his fingers and watched the sand exit his hand.

"Do you think it's weird?" she wondered aloud.

"I don't know," he shrugged. "The two-women part doesn't seem all that strange to me. Most of the people I know are like that. But the baby thing's a little different."

"How so?"

Theron squinted out over the lake. "You and Jane really want this baby, and Dar's looking forward to it too. And I know Keely's excited about it even though she doesn't show it. Nobody's ever wanted me," he lamented. "Not even Dar."

"Come on now, Theron. That's not fair."

"I know, I know," he rolled his eyes. "Keely gave me the lecture already this morning."

"Theron!"

"Okay, I'm sorry," he apologized. "But it just sucks, you know? My mother took off just after I was born, and my dad sure as hell doesn't want me. What am I supposed to do? Go back and live with my grandparents again?"

Beth didn't know what to say.

"I know nobody believes me, but Meg hates me and even Gwen doesn't really like me. She's kind of like a big sister. I know she loves me and everything, but mostly she thinks I'm a pain in the ass. It's different with Dar. She cares about me and talks to me. She's kind of like my best friend."

"And what about Keely? You'd be living with her too."

Theron shrugged. "Keely's cool."

Beth smiled.

"And you and Jane are okay too."

"Thank you, Theron," she accepted his huge compliment graciously.

Theron looked out over the lake again. "Don't ever tell Dar this, but I wish she was my mother."

Beth wasn't surprised he felt that way but was amazed he'd actually managed to say it.

Keely got to her feet. "I'm going with you."

"There's no need to. I'm just going to drive Theron home and talk to Gwen for a while. Why don't you just stay and enjoy the sun for the day?"

She shook her head. "You'll be tired and upset, and I don't want you driving back alone."

"You're being ridiculous," Darla objected. "I'll be fine."

Keely retreated to lean against the kitchen counter.

"What's the matter?" Darla read the signs.

Keely looked at her feet. "I know this sounds kind of stupid, but I miss taking care of you. Pretty soon you'll be able to do everything on your own."

Darla smiled.

"You don't need me any more," she out-and-out whined.

Darla put her arms around her. "Oh, Keely," she cooed. "I'll always need you."

"I'm surprised they're not back yet."

Jane smiled. "Maybe they stopped to melt the ice cream again."

Beth laughed. It was a plausible explanation. "What do you think is going to happen?"

"Let's put it this way," Jane grinned. "I wonder how Theron feels about babysitting?"

"I didn't think Gwen would say it was okay so easily."

Keely nodded. She didn't either.

Darla sighed. "It would be a hell of a lot simpler if I didn't love the little shit so much."

She couldn't disagree.

"Now I really don't know what to do."

Keely smiled. "Yes, you do."

October

KEELY TIPTOED INTO the bedroom. She sat down cautiously on the edge of the bed. Darla opened her eyes and smiled at her.

"What time is it?" she sleepily inquired.

Keely winced guiltily. "One-thirty. I'm sorry," she apologized. "I suppose the shower woke you?"

Darla nodded.

"I wouldn't have bothered taking one, but the job site's a sea of mud," she explained. "I was absolutely filthy."

"You must be exhausted," Darla worried about her eighteen-hour day. "Are you okay?"

"I've still got all ten toes and nine-and-a-bit fingers," she sighed. "But I'm getting too old for this shit."

Darla smiled and lifted the duvet for her to crawl in.

"No baby yet?" she checked.

Darla shook her head. "And she's not in the least happy about it either," she smiled.

"Brock told me today that Cindy's pregnant," Keely relayed. "She's due in early May."

"Brock must be thrilled."

"Ecstatic," Keely confirmed. "He was on cloud nine all day."

"Are you going to get home in reasonable time tomorrow night?"

"I'll be home by six," Keely promised.

Darla snuggled up beside her. "I miss you lately."

"I miss you too."

"Are you really working all these late hours or are you out running around on me?"

Keely laughed heartily. Darla licked her ear playfully.

"Just how tired are you?"

Keely smiled. "That depends. What did you have in mind?"

"Did you say anything to Dar yet?"

Beth shook her head. "And I haven't mentioned it to Keely either."

Jane sat on the edge of the bed and kicked her shoes off. She was sure that over the course of the last eight hours her feet had at least tripled in size.

"I think we should do it together," Beth decided. "And maybe not for a little while. Keely seems kind of stressed out lately."

Jane reached down in a vain attempt to rub her aching arches. Beth took the matter in hand immediately.

"God, that feels great," she erupted ecstatically.

"Almost as good as sex?" Beth teased.

Jane laughed. "At this point, probably better." She sprawled back on the bed and closed her eyes, more than willing to give in to the distraction.

"So what do you think of my suggestion?" Beth got back on topic again.

"What suggestion?" she mumbled groggily.

"That we ask Keely and Dar to be Jane Junior's guardians sometime when we're all together, but not until after the baby's born?" she repeated.

"Mmm," she murmured.

Beth lay down beside her and smiled contentedly. A nap seemed as good a way as any to celebrate the start of Jane's maternity leave.

"Keely's not here," he relayed. "She left quite a while ago."

Brock's disclosure was met with silence on the other end of the phone.

"You're not worried, are you?"

"No. Not really," Darla lied efficiently. "She's just a little later than she said she'd be."

"I'm sure she just stopped to do something on her way home," he reassured her.

Her stomach did a flip-flop at the thought. "You're probably right," she feigned consolation. "Thanks, Brock."

"That's a nice colour."

Keely turned with a start. She didn't know Beth was standing there.

"Where's Dar?"

"She's gone over to Gwen's with Theron," Keely relayed. "I didn't want her hanging around here in the paint fumes."

"I'll go and change so I can help you," Beth offered.

"Don't bother," she shook her suggestion off. "I don't mind. It gives me something to do."

Beth nodded. Keely just wasn't herself lately.

"Is Jane sleeping?"

Beth nodded again. She stood in the doorway watching Keely for a moment or two longer before entering the room. In some ways it seemed like a million years ago and in other ways it was just as if it was yesterday that it had been her bedroom. And now what had originally been Dar's guest room, and then her room, and then when they finished the attic, their guest room, was going through yet another transformation. It would be Dar's new office tomorrow, probably by no later than noon.

Keely set her roller in the paint tray and stepped back to admire her work.

"It looks really good," Beth complimented her.

Keely shrugged and sat down on the step stool.

"Are you okay?" Beth checked.

"I'm fine," Keely replied. "I just feel a little out of it these days."

Beth nodded. She could relate quite directly.

"How about you?"

Beth smiled. "I've got more than my fair share of neuroses."

"Such as?" Keely prompted.

"Such as my mixed emotions about having moved, or my ever-present case of cold feet about becoming mommy number two to Jane Junior," she laughed. "Or my paranoia about screwing things up with Jane, just to mention a few."

Keely chuckled appreciatively.

Beth grew suddenly serious again. "I love you," she said.

Her words bushwhacked Keely out of nowhere.

"I realized the other day it's been a long time since I've said that to you."

Keely smiled at her. "I love you too."

"You know if you ever need to talk or anything ...."

"I'll come downstairs looking for you," Keely finished the sentence so she didn't have to.

"Dar. Hi. What a nice surprise. Come on in."

"I hope you don't mind my dropping by, but I was in the neighbourhood," she lied.

Cindy smiled at her pleasantly. "I was just finishing up in the studio. Why don't you keep me company while I clean up?"

Darla followed her through the kitchen to the back room. "I hope I'm not disturbing you?"

"Not at all," Cindy assured her. "I'll just be a couple of minutes and then we can sit down and have a coffee."

Darla wandered about the room enjoying the ambience while Cindy returned to her task of cleaning brushes by the sink. Darla stopped by the drawing table to admire the bright watercolours drying there.

"What are you working on?"

"Just a few illustrations for a kids book again."

"Another collaboration with your sister?" Darla presumed.

Cindy nodded and wiped her hands on the back of her jeans.

"What's it about?"

"A little boy whose mother has breast cancer," she smiled sheepishly.

Darla was genuinely pleased.

"Ready for that coffee now?"

"Sure," she agreed. "But actually, if you don't mind I'd rather have tea. My taste buds seem to have changed since the chemotherapy."

"Tea it is," Cindy decreed and proceeded immediately to the kitchen. "So how have you been feeling?" she inquired.

"Very well," Darla smiled. "Over the last couple of weeks I've actually started to feel like myself again."

Cindy rummaged through the cupboards, hoping like hell they actually had some tea.

"I hear congratulations are in order," Darla offered.

Cindy beamed. "Brock's really paranoid because of my age," she relayed. "I figure, what the hell," she giggled. "Accidents happen. I'm not the first woman to have an oops at forty."

Darla chuckled approvingly. Cindy sat down across from her at the table.

"So?" she prompted pointedly.

"I wanted to talk to you about Keely," Darla admitted.

Cindy smiled and nodded. She wasn't exactly surprised.

"Has she seemed ..." Darla paused, searching for the right word, "... funny lately?"

"A little distant maybe," she gauged.

Darla nodded. Beth had used the term preoccupied. "Any idea as to why?"

Cindy shook her head. "No. Not really. But you've had a pretty busy household lately."

Darla smiled at the understatement.

"My best guess would be that she's having a tough time adjusting to all the changes."

Darla nodded again. That's what both Beth and Jane had said. And who could blame Keely, what with Beth and Jane moving out and Theron moving in? In many ways it seemed like a plausible interpretation, except it in no way explained her mysterious disappearances or why it felt like she was just going through the motions when they made love lately.

"You don't think it's that simple, do you?" Cindy guessed.

Darla shook her head.

"What do you think is going on then?"

Darla took a deep breath. "I think Keely's having an affair."

"I feel like a bloody beached whale," she complained. "Can't we just stay in for my birthday?"

Beth smiled at her Jane. "We're just going upstairs to Dar and Keely's. Surely you can make it that far?"

Jane bent over and grudgingly crammed her swollen and aching feet into her slippers. And then she just sat there.

"Come on, you two," Beth encouraged her again.

She didn't move a muscle.

"Jane?"

"I think we might have to put the party on hold, Beth," she struggled for her breath. "Unless I miss my guess, I'd say my birthday present is on her way."

Brock watched Keely replace the receiver. She had the strangest look on her face.

"Was that Beth?"

Keely nodded.

"Jane had her baby," he presumed.

She nodded again.

"Is everything okay?"

"Fine," Keely confirmed.

"A boy or a girl?" he checked.

"A boy. Eight pounds something."

"What did they name him?"

Keely shrugged. "They haven't decided yet."

Brock didn't know what to think. He thought she'd be a least a little excited about it or something. "Are you disappointed because it's a boy?"

Keely shook her head. She couldn't care less.

"Well, what's wrong then?"

"Nothing," she snapped.

"You don't seem very happy about it."

"I'm fucking thrilled," she seethed.

"Could have fooled me."

"What the hell do you want from me?" she yelled. "Jane had her baby. Good for her. Your wife is pregnant.

Good for you too. There. Are you satisfied?"

Brock watched her stomp off, totally mystified.

Beth sat down tentatively on the edge of the bed and kissed her on the forehead.

"You can do better than that," she smiled.

Beth proceeded to do so immediately.

"I love you."

"I love you too," Beth replied.

Jane picked up her hand. "Are you really disappointed it wasn't a girl?"

Beth shook her head. "I got exactly what I wanted. You're both okay."

Jane smiled. "But are you?"

Beth studied the bassinet beside the bed carefully. "I'm a little blown away," she confessed. "I didn't expect to feel like this."

"Like what?"

"Like he's part mine," she twitched uncomfortably.

"But he is," Jane replied evenly. "He's your son too."

Beth considered it silently.

"Too much responsibility?"

Beth shook her head.

"What then?"

Beth smiled. "Sometimes I just can't believe how much I love you."

"Are you going to grow your hair long again?"

Darla rinsed her mouth and looked into the mirror above the sink. She considered the short silver curls that had taken the place of her straight, shoulder-length hair. "I don't know, big guy. What do you think?"

Theron studied her reflection thoughtfully. "I like it like this," he decided.

Darla smiled. It was unanimous. Keely did too. She stopped short at the thought. "Do you think it makes me look older?" she reconsidered.

"I don't know," he waffled. "I don't think so, but maybe."

Darla screwed up her face. Maybe it was time to start colouring it again. Looking a little younger in Keely's eyes certainly couldn't hurt.

"What time is Keely getting home?" he intruded on her latest round of insecurities.

Darla glanced at her watch. "Any minute now," she realized. "Go and put on something clean, with no holes in it, and preferably not jeans."

"That might be a bit of a problem," he schemed. "I really need to do laundry."

"Are your dress pants dirty too?" she was on to him.

Theron screwed up his face. "They make me look faggy."

Darla shot him a look.

"Not that there's anything wrong with that, but I really hate them," he scrambled to appease. "Can't I borrow something of Keely's?"

"All right then," Darla caved in. "Go and look in the closet. But for heaven's sake, put some underwear on. You know how that makes her crazy."

Theron disappeared, one happy camper. He'd gotten exactly what he wanted.

"Who are those from?"

Beth picked the card out of the lavish bouquet. "Well, fuck me!" She covered her mouth with her hand immediately at the pained looked that appeared on both Jane and her father's face. "Pardon me," she apologized, "but sometimes I can't believe just how effective the jungle drums are."

"Who are they from?" Jane asked again.

"Louise."

"Well, fuck me," Peter agreed.

Keely sat down on the edge of the tub and pulled her socks off. "Have you been to see him yet?"

Darla shook her head. "I thought I'd wait for you."

Keely nodded and stood to drop her pants.

"Rough day?"

"Uh-huh," she confirmed.

Darla observed her closely.

"I'm okay," Keely intercepted. "I'm just a little tired. A shower will make me feel better."

Darla knew full well she was lying.

"Why don't you go and check on Theron?" she diverted her attention skilfully. "Last time I saw him, he had half of our closet heaped on the bed."

Darla hesitated uncertainly.

"I won't be long," Keely promised and ducked into the shower immediately.

The hot water made Keely feel ten years younger. By the time she finished, she wasn't a day over 160.

"He's adorable," she gushed.

Jane and Beth glowed proudly. Maureen looked at her daughter expectantly.

"Oh, I'm sorry," Beth's manners kicked in. "This is Jane's father, Peter Tolliver. And this is my mother, Maureen Campbell."

"Pleased to meet you," they mutually beamed.

Maureen turned her attention back to the bundle of joy. "Come to Grandma," she staked her claim.

Jane gave up possession immediately. Beth had been worrying about her mother's reaction needlessly.

"He looks just like you," Grandma Campbell addressed Grandpa Tolliver. "No wonder they gave him your name."

Beth rolled her eyes. She hated to admit it, but once again her Jane was right. As sick and twisted as it was, their parents really were a match made in heaven. Jane looked at her and winked.

"I told you it would be a boy," Theron expounded.

"That's right. You did," Jane agreed.

Keely handed Baby Tolliver awkwardly over to his Aunt Dar. "Does he have a name yet?"

Beth smiled. "Walter Peter Campbell Tolliver. We're going to call him Cam."

"Wally would be thrilled," Darla approved entirely.

Beth nodded. "It was Jane's idea."

"Who's Wally?" Theron asked.

"He was a friend of Beth's who died a couple of years ago," Darla provided.

"And Peter's my father's name," Jane further illuminated.

Theron nodded. "Campbell's Beth's last name. Why would you name him that?"

"For legal reasons," Darla explained. "I think it's a lovely name. Don't you?" she prodded him.

Theron nodded. He really didn't think so, but he wasn't saying anything.

"Would you like to hold him?" Jane asked.

He looked at Darla uncertainly. She nodded and motioned to him. He sat down in the chair.

"Hi, Cam," he greeted him. "I'm Theron. I'm sort of your brother or cousin or something."

"Instead of freezing your ass off, why don't you get in here?"

Keely looked at her guiltily. It was two-thirty in the morning. She didn't think she'd get caught. She dropped her cigarette to the deck and stepped on it.

"If you're going to smoke, the least you could do is use an ashtray," Darla muttered disapprovingly.

Keely picked up the butt and followed her inside to deposit it in the kitchen garbage can.

"Sit down," Darla directed. "I want to talk to you."

Keely sat obediently at the kitchen table. She really wasn't looking forward to the upcoming lecture on the evils of smoking.

"Do you want some tea?" Darla offered.

Keely shook her head. Darla went about making it anyway. She eventually joined Keely at the table, carrying an ashtray and a steaming cup.

"You might as well smoke inside," she decided. "You've been doing it for weeks anyway."

Keely looked at her totally surprised. She didn't think she knew.

"Go ahead and have one if you'd like," she granted her permission outright.

Keely shook her head.

Darla took a sip of her tea. "Are you just going to sit there, or do you think you might talk to me?"

"I'm sorry about the smoking," she apologized dutifully.

"Your smoking is the least of my worries right now," Darla replied.

"Is something wrong?" she panicked.

"I don't know, Keely. You tell me."

Keely looked at her blankly.

"You're the one who's been pulling disappearing acts lately."

Keely sighed wearily. There was no point in trying to hide it any more. "I've gone back to AA," she divulged reluctantly. "I've been going to a lot of meetings lately."

Darla stared at her in disbelief. "Why didn't you tell me?"

"Because I didn't want to upset or worry you."

Darla shook her head at the irony. "How much worse do you think it would have been to tell me than to leave me guessing? The last few days I've been going crazy."

"I'm sorry," Keely apologized guiltily.

"I was scared you were having an affair," she admitted ever so softly.

"An affair? Oh, Jesus, Dar," she laughed. "How could you even think that?"

"That's what Cindy said to me."

"You talked to Cindy?"

Darla nodded. "And to Beth and Jane and Brock. Nobody knew what was going on with you. They all guessed that you were upset about all the changes around here. Is that what has made you want to start drinking again?"

Keely averted her gaze immediately.

"Let me help you," Darla urged. "Stop trying to handle everything on your own."

Keely struggled against her tears valiantly.

"Please, Keely," she begged. "Whatever it is, you can tell me."

Keely swallowed. "I'm afraid you're going to die," she started to cry.

"Oh, Keely," she sighed. She was so busy suspecting the worst, she'd missed the obvious.

"I can't get it out of my mind," Keely sobbed. "It's the first thing I think about when I wake up in the morning and the last thing before I go to sleep. Everything reminds me that at any moment you could get sick again. The first thing that struck me when Beth called this morning was that you might never get to see Cam grow up."

Darla reached across the table to touch her hand. "I'm not going anywhere, Keely," she promised.

Keely wiped her nose on the back of her hand. "You don't know that," she sniffled. "You're just saying it."

"Keely, I feel fine. Really."

"You felt fine last year too," she reminded her.

Darla paused to regroup. This wasn't getting anywhere.

"It's just so unfair," Keely muttered. "Everybody around us is getting everything they could even think to ask for, and at any moment I could lose the only thing I've ever really wanted."

"You mean me?"

Keely nodded and swiped at her nose in annoyance again.

Darla considered her strategy carefully. "You're right," she agreed. "Someday I am going to die and it will probably be long before you do," she replied calmly. "That's not anything new, Keely. I am almost twelve years older than you."

Keely shook her head. She wasn't listening.

"I wish you'd stop viewing the cancer so negatively," she tried.

Keely looked at her incredulously. "It's a little hard to see it any other way, if you ask me."

Darla smiled.

"What are you smiling for?" she snapped testily.

"I was smiling because you seem to have conveniently forgotten that if it wasn't for the cancer, you and I would probably never have spoken again."

"That was the first time around," she reacted defensively.

"Yes, it was," Darla agreed. "What makes you so certain something good won't come of this time too?"

Keely considered it silently.

"In fact, I'd say it already has," she upped the ante. "Theron certainly wouldn't have moved in here if we hadn't gotten to know each other so well when I was sick, and I dare say Jane wouldn't have touched living here with a ten-foot pole any other way. And if I didn't have cancer, who's to say we'd even have run into Jane that night on the street? Maybe she and Beth would never have gotten back together again, and if that hadn't happened, then for sure we'd never have even met Cam."

Keely closed her eyes. She was suddenly very tired.

"You can't just wish my having cancer away and keep everything else the same," Darla persisted. "Everything would be different. You, me, everything."

Keely dropped her head into her hands. If wishes were horses, then beggars would ride.

"Even if I died tomorrow, my second round of cancer would have already brought about some pretty wonderful things."

She gave up the struggle and just let herself cry.

"I love you," Darla tried.

Keely looked up into the warmth of her eyes. "But I'm not ready for you to die."

"That's okay, Keely," she smiled. "Neither am I."

December

"THERON WANTS A motorcycle for Christmas," Darla announced.

Beth laughed. "What did Keely say?"

"I think her exact words were, 'no fucking way.' As far as Keely's concerned, one motorcycle per household is already too many."

Beth didn't exactly disagree.

"What did you get Jane for Christmas?" she wondered idly.

"We're doing the matching ring thing."

"Finally getting married, are we?" she teased.

Beth just beamed. Darla went back to watching Cam sleep.

"What are you getting Keely?"

"That's for me to know and for you and Keely to find out," she replied evasively.

"Come on, Dar. Give me a hint."

"What I'm hopefully going to give her doesn't cost anything."

Beth mulled that one over for a while. "You canned the idea of the handcuffs then?" she trolled for another clue.

Darla laughed. "That was just a stocking stuffer anyway."

Beth was completely stymied.

"I did remember to get the extra-large strap-on dildo for Jane though," she tormented her wickedly.

Beth shot her a look.

Darla reconsidered. "Or should I give it to you?"

She didn't have to dodge any flying debris this time. Darla had played it safe. She was holding Cam.

Darla shifted over to the passenger seat of the car. "You drive," she decided.

Keely was pleasantly surprised. The first snowstorm of the year was usually Dar's favourite excuse to drive like a total maniac. She started the Mercedes and pulled out into traffic.

"I got my test results today."

Keely's knuckles turned white as she gripped the steering wheel. "What did they say?" she braved.

"That my right breast is definitely nowhere to be found and my left breast isn't the same tit it used to be. Oh, and most of my lymph nodes are missing in action too."

Keely turned the corner mechanically.

"According to all reports, however, I do still have all my bones and my liver is right where it's supposed to be."

Keely pulled up to the red light and turned to look at her.

"It's okay," Darla beamed. "Everything came back clean. There's absolutely no cancer to be found anywhere."

Keely put the car in park and threw her arms around her.

"Merry Christmas, Keely," Darla wished her. "I love you."